"Are you okay?"

"Yes. Fine." She smiled.

"Going in?" he asked with what sounded like amusement in his voice.

"O   , ex   ha

W th   d how tall he actually was and how his lean frame belied the power beneath.

Avery swallowed and stepped around him. Her heart banged mercilessly as she walked to her front door with Rafe a half step behind.

She turned. "Thanks so much for inviting me tonight. I had a great time."

His eyes picked up the light from the moon and seemed to sparkle. He grinned, leaned down and placed a featherlight kiss on her forehead. "Good night. Rest well. I hope you don't mind if I call on you again."

"You're going to fly all the way from Louisiana to DC just to see me?"

"My family has a place in Arlington, Virginia. When I have good reason, I stay there." He leveled his gaze on her. "Do I have good reason?"

"You might," she managed to say.

Dear Reader,

Throughout the Lawson-family series, Rafe Lawson has been that elusive, dangerous, sexy shadow that readers were dying to discover more about. *Surrender to Me* is his story.

To be honest, I was terrified to finally write about Rafe. The stakes seemed so high. But I put on my big-girl pants and dug in. The shroud of mystery around the man was slowly pulled back, and I know that the revelations will surprise as well as endear him even further in your hearts.

Rafe is complicated, a confirmed bachelor with looks, money and charisma sprinkled with a heavy dose of Southern gentleman, and it takes an extraordinary woman like Avery Richards to make him realize that surrendering is not a weakness. Creating Avery, I knew that she needed to be really different. So she is a Secret Service agent skilled at looking for anything out of place. Avery is fearless and focused even as she has her own internal enemies to deal with. I hope that you will laugh, cry, scream and root for Rafe and Avery. I know that I did!

I love to hear from readers. You can always find me on Facebook; please join my fan club at Facebook.com/donnahillfans for updates on new projects and sneak peeks at upcoming works. Also, follow me on Twitter, @donnahill.

As always, thank you all for twenty-five years of support!

Until next time,

Donna

SURRENDER TO *Me*

DONNA HILL

H HARLEQUIN® KIMANI™ ROMANCE

Recycling programs
for this product may
not exist in your area.

ISBN-13: 978-0-373-86511-6

Surrender to Me

Printed in U.S.A.

Donna Hill published her first novel in 1990. She now has more than eighty titles in print. Three of her novels have been adapted for television. She has received numerous awards and recognition for her wide body of work. In her other life, Donna is an assistant professor of English at Medgar Evers College in Brooklyn, New York, and an adjunct professor at Baruch College and Essex County College. She has an MFA in creative writing from Goddard College. Donna lives in Brooklyn with her family. Visit her website at www.donnahill.com.

Books by Donna Hill
Harlequin Kimani Romance

If I Were Your Woman
After Dark
Sex and Lies
Seduction and Lies
Temptation and Lies
Longing and Lies
Private Lessons
Spend My Life with You
Secret Attraction
Sultry Nights
Everything Is You
Mistletoe, Baby
The Way You Love Me
My Love at Last
For the Love of You
Surrender to Me

Visit the Author Profile page
at Harlequin.com for more titles.

This novel is lovingly dedicated to my tireless editor, Glenda Howard, who continues to champion my work.

Chapter 1

A warm leg brushed against his. Rafe Lawson glanced over his shoulder through dark eyes still lazy with sleep. He blinked slowly in the dim light of early morning, bringing the body next to him into focus. The night before began to come back to him in brief snapshots. His grandfather Clive's birthday party. Bourbon. Music. Beautiful women.

He gently lifted the pale blue sheet that covered her body and peeked beneath. Hmm. Very nice. But for the life of him he couldn't remember her name. And she definitely was not the woman he'd dreamed about all night—the woman he'd met at the party.

They'd only had a few moments to talk. She was part of the Secret Service detail that was assigned to the vice president, who'd made a surprise visit for his old friend's birthday. *Avery!* That was her name. *The woman from last night.*

The unnamed woman in his bed moaned softly and he felt her lush body stretch against him. He eased out of bed and strode to the adjoining bathroom.

Rafe leaned on the sink and assessed his reflection in the mirror. The residue from his night of partying was barely evident beyond the five-o'clock shadow that outlined his jaw.

At thirty-six, his body still bounced back from the wear and tear he subjected it to; whether tearing up the highways on his motorcycle, hours in the gym or nights of indulgence in alcohol and women. He knew, however, that his often wild lifestyle couldn't be maintained forever. He lived for the adrenaline rush of living on the edge, on his own terms, even to the dismay of family and friends. He did it as much to amuse himself as to piss off his powerful father.

He backed away from the all-knowing mirror and turned on the shower full-blast in the hope that his head would clear about the events that led to the woman in his bed.

By the time he turned off the taps he remembered— and it wasn't good. The lovely lady was Shante Thornton, who worked for his sister Dominique. He muttered a curse while he knotted a towel around his waist. Back in front of the mirror he wiped the fogged glass with a cloth. His face appeared haloed by the mist. "You're an idiot," he grumbled.

When Rafe returned, Shante was sitting on the side of the bed with the sheet pulled up around her. She glanced quickly at him, turned away and clutched the sheet in her fist, but not before he registered the look of uncertainty and maybe embarrassment in her eyes. Without makeup and the fancy gown that was now tossed on an armchair, he could see how young she was. Not underage jail potential, but younger than the women he was accustomed to dealing with. There was a vulnerability that engulfed her like the scent of great sex that still lingered in the room.

He may be a womanizer in the eyes of some, but the truth was he loved women, adored them. He cherished the bodies of women, the soft curves of their shoulders and hips, the sexy spot behind the ear right down to the lobe, and the allure of the collarbone and the lovely space where he could dip his tongue and feel the pulse, and the sensual pull of a woman's breasts when he held them in his palms was always exciting. Women's bodies fascinated him and he made it his duty to explore, awaken and satisfy. He treasured their minds equally, and there was nothing more singularly sexy than an intelligent woman. But in every instance he treated them all with equal doses of charm and respect—a mantra that he lived by. Unfortunately, it had gotten him into more trouble than he needed on occasion.

"Mornin', sugah," he said while he crossed the room. He sat beside her and felt her tense. "Sleep okay?"

She barely nodded her head. Rafe smiled and that seemed to break the ice.

"I haven't slept that good in ages."

"It's the sheets," he teased.

Shante laughed softly.

"There're fresh towels in the bathroom." He stood. "I'll fix us some breakfast. Bacon and eggs cool?"

"Sounds great."

"Coffee? Tea? Juice?"

"Coffee," she asked more than stated.

"Got it." He left and as he reached the door he heard her get up from the bed and scurry into the bathroom. Modesty was actually an admirable trait.

He deftly threw together his morning-after omelet special of cheddar and sharp cheeses, green and red peppers and diced bits of ham mixed with a dash of milk to keep the eggs light and fluffy; a trick he'd learned from his mom. He hummed while he worked and in between every other note he thought about or saw an image of Avery. Rarely did one woman leave that kind of impression on him. He was used to easily seducing the woman that he wanted; a full-on Lawson press. Not this time. He frowned as he replayed their brief encounter.

He'd noticed her the moment she walked in and it was clear, even in an eye-popping black gown, that her presence was more than an invited guest. He could tell by the way her gaze covertly scanned the room, noted the exits and followed at a discreet distance from the vice president that she was part of his security detail— Secret Service. He had an image of a .22 strapped to her inner thigh.

Unlike many highbrow gatherings of politicos and the like that were too reserved for his tastes, a Lawson party was the real deal full of loud laughter, louder conversations and the music to go with it. So of course he had to get particularly close to talk to her.

He gave her time to assess the layout before he approached. He came alongside her. "Can I get you anything?"

She turned cinnamon-brown eyes on him, fanned by long curved lashes. Her smile was practiced, distant, but Rafe didn't miss the rapid beat of her pulse in the dip of her throat that belied her cool exterior. Her sleek right brow rose in question as she took him in with one long glance.

"Clearly you're not one of the waitstaff," she said with a hint of amusement in her voice.

"Rafe Lawson."

Her eyes widened for a split second. "Oh, the scandalous one."

He dramatically pressed his hand to his chest. "Guilty as charged, cher, but I have perfectly reasonable explanations for everything."

Her eyes sparkled when the light hit them. "I'm sure you do, Mr. Lawson."

"So what can I get for you that won't interfere with you being on duty?"

She tensed ever so slightly.

"Trust me. I've grown up in this life. I can spot Secret Service a mile away. Although I must admit that you bring class to the dark suits and Ray-Bans."

She glanced past him to where her colleague stood near the vice president. In one fluid motion she gave a barely imperceptible lift of her chin, a quick scan of the room and said, "Nice to meet you," as she made a move to leave.

He held her bare arm. "Tell me your name," he commanded almost in her ear. He inhaled her, felt the slight shiver that gripped her.

"Avery."

Rafe released her and followed the dangerously low-cut back of her dress until she was out of sight.

"Smells delicious."

Rafe blinked, glanced over his shoulder. Definitely cute, but she wasn't Avery. He took two plates from the overhead cabinet and set them on the table. "Help yourself to coffee."

"Thanks."

He spooned the eggs onto a platter and added the bacon. "Toast?"

"No. I'm fine with this."

Rafe poured himself a glass of orange juice, straddled the stool and sat. "How long have you been working with my sister, six months?"

"Just about."

He watched her over the rim of his glass as she tried to remain ladylike when she took a half spoonful of eggs and one strip of bacon when he knew damn well she had to be starving because he was.

He lifted the serving spoon from the platter, loaded it with eggs and plopped it on her plate, followed by two strips of bacon.

"We've already experienced carnal knowledge, honey, no point in putting on a show now. Eat like you mean it." He winked and filled his plate.

"I...want you to know that... I don't do this."

"What's that, Shante, eat breakfast?"

She sputtered a laugh. "No. I mean...spend the night with a man the first time I meet him."

He chewed thoughtfully. "Hmm. Okay." He smiled, slow and deliberate. "I consider it an honor, cher." He watched her sandy brown skin flush then tucked a strand of hair behind her ears. His fingers instinctively caressed the smooth lock. "Eat up. I'll drop you home before I take care of the rest of my day."

* * *

Rafe preferred the black Range Rover for his everyday use rather than either of his two cars or his motorcycle. Plus the roominess gave him an artificial sense of distance when he knew it would be the last official time he'd drop a woman at her door. The intimacy of a car made parting more difficult.

"Thanks for a great evening…and breakfast," Shante said. She smiled shyly.

"It was my pleasure." He remotely unlocked the doors, got out and came around to her side. He held her hand to help her out.

Shante glanced up at him and he knew this was the "I'll call you" moment that wouldn't happen.

Rafe leaned down and placed a long, tender kiss on her forehead, ran his thumb along the line of her jaw, turned and got back in the Rover.

A spark of guilt ignited with the turn of the key. It always did at times like this. He checked his mirrors and slowly pulled off.

No sooner had he driven away and gotten back on the main road than his cell phone rang. He pressed an icon on the dash and his sister Dominique's voice came through the speaker.

"Tell me that you did not take Shante home with you last night."

"Well hello, Dom, and how are you today?"

"Don't play with me, Raford Lawson."

Anytime his family used his full name he knew he had to brace for the inevitable tongue-lashing. "Okay, I won't tell you."

"Damn it, Rafe!"

"What? She's grown and so am I."

"That's not the point and you know it."

"No. I don't. Why don't you enlighten me like I know you want to do."

Dominique sighed heavily. "You run through women like socks, Rafe. Shante's a nice girl and—"

"And I treated her like a nice *woman*. There is no way that she could say anything different."

"I know that. That's the problem. You treat them all like princesses and then poof, move on. Telephone book of broken hearts."

"Bit of an exaggeration, sis." He turned onto the street where his club was located.

"We work together, Rafe. I don't need her grilling me about you and whining in my ear when you don't call."

"What makes you think I won't call?"

"Will you?" She pushed out a frustrated breath when silence hung between them. "Aggh. If you weren't my brother…"

Rafe chuckled. "Love you, too, sis. Gotta go."

"Fine. Try to stay out of trouble."

"Always." He pulled into his parking spot. He disconnected the call and cut the engine.

Dominique, unlike her twin Desiree, had no problem saying what was on her mind regardless of how her remarks fell on the ears and souls of her target. She'd softened somewhat since she got together with Trevor Jackson. But even he couldn't always keep the lid on Dominique. Now that their eldest sister, Lee Ann, was married and expecting, Dominique took on the role as head Lawson woman in charge.

He had to laugh. As much as he loved his siblings they could be a bit much at times, never mind that he was the eldest son. With three females, he and his younger brother Justin didn't stand a chance.

Rafe entered the club through the back door. He flipped on lights as he strolled through. No matter how many times he crossed the gray marble floors, walked behind the circular bar or looked out onto the eclectic crowd that packed the house night after night, he still got that rush. This was his, the one thing separate and apart from the Lawson legacy of money, politics and backdoor deals, much to his father's horror.

From the time he was old enough to walk and talk, his father, Branford, began to groom him for politics. And from the moment Rafe was old enough to think for himself he resented what his father wanted for him. The last footsteps he wanted to walk in were his father's and that caused a rift between father and son that had spanned the better part of his adult life.

Fortunately, his sister Lee Ann married Sterling, a senator, and Justin had taken up the Lawson mantel, gotten his law degree and had begun to carve a name for himself in civil liberties law with his private law firm. It was only a matter of time before he pursued public office.

Rafe went behind the bar and fixed himself a quick shot of bourbon. Sure it was early, but what the hell. He placed his phone on the bar top. 11:30. His staff would arrive soon to prep for the five o'clock opening. He sipped his drink, picked up his phone and called his brother.

Justin answered on the third ring. "You're on speaker so don't say anything crazy." He chuckled.

"Thanks for the heads-up."

"I didn't see you leave last night."

"Yeah, kinda flew under the radar."

"Hmm, I know what that means. So…what's up?"

"Look, there was this woman there last night…"

"Oh really?" Justin teased.

"This is different," Rafe said, pacing in front of the bar.

"What do you mean?"

Rafe paused a moment, trying to piece what was running through his head together. "I don't know, man. I saw her and…anyway, she's been on mind."

"Okay… I know you're not asking for my advice." He chuckled.

"Not exactly. More like a favor."

"Shoot."

"All I know is her name is Avery and she works for the Secret Service. She was on the VP detail."

"Whoa. Okay. And…"

"And I need you to use some of your connections to find out her last name and how I can reach her. I'm sure Dad knows, but he's the last person I'd ask."

"Hmm. I'll see what I can find out. Is it really that important?"

"Yeah, it is."

"Don't think I've heard that tone in your voice before. This is new."

"Guess it is," he said, the realization hitting him. He took a swallow of his drink. Frowned.

"Actually, I get it. Ran into this woman weeks ago at a bar downtown. Couldn't shake her, and damn if she wasn't the bartender at Granddad's party."

"What! But you were with what's-her-name. The one none of us like."

Justin grumbled deep in his throat. "Yes, the situation got a little awkward. But at least I know where she works. It wasn't until last night that she actually knew who I was."

"What does that mean? You been seeing her in disguise? Using a false name?" He chuckled.

"Naw. I just never told her I was a Lawson."

"For obvious reasons. I get it. Say no more. But now that she knows what's your next move?"

"I plan to see her again. There's this connection. Ya know?"

"Yeah, bro, I think I do."

The front door opened and the club manager Carlos walked in with Paul the house chef and Rafe's favorite two waitresses Simone and Leslie right behind them.

"Gotta run. Duty calls."

"Yeah, me, too. Meeting a client."

"So you'll check that out for me?"

"No doubt."

"Cool. And, J…"

"Yeah…?"

"Good luck with your lady friend."

"Thanks."

"What's her name by the way?"

"Bailey. Bailey Sinclair."

"Bailey. I like it." He chuckled. "Be easy."

"You, too."

Rafe pocketed his phone and greeted his staff, all the while wondering how long it would take Justin to find out what he wanted to know.

Chapter 2

Avery Richards planted her feet, aimed her Glock and fired six rounds in rapid succession. She extracted the earplugs and removed the protective goggles. The paper target floated toward her like a ghost in a bad B movie. Five to the chest and one right between the eyes.

"Not bad."

Avery gave a cursory glance and chose to ignore the comment.

Mike Stone, often her detail partner and unrequited suitor, stepped into the booth next to hers. She wouldn't characterize their relationship as adversarial but it was often tense. Mostly because Avery was damned good at every aspect of her job, she had seniority and she didn't fall under his questionable charms.

Mike was accustomed to having what and who he wanted. The fact that he couldn't live out what he believed to be his manifest destiny with Avery irked him to no end. It didn't, however, stop him from challenging her whenever it suited him. Quite frankly she was tired of his bullshit male ego and planned to ask to be reassigned.

She'd been hired under the first female head of the Secret Service. Avery didn't have the same rapport with her replacement and she didn't want to play the victim card. But the fact was she didn't trust Mike and that could prove tragic if placed in a life or death situation. She didn't want to pull her trump card and ask for favors from her senator father. She needed to work this out on her own. That or simply shoot Mike and put them both out of their misery.

"Ever think about just wounding?" He put on his goggles.

"You. I have, yes."

He laughed and plugged his ears. "Dead suspects tell no tales."

She rolled her eyes, holstered her weapon and detached her target sheet. "Have a good day, Mike," she said. The drip of sarcasm pooled at her feet.

The sound of gunfire followed her out of the target range.

When Avery pushed through the heavy steel door and entered the long corridor that led to a row of offices, she ran into her friend Kerry Holt.

She and Kerry had trained together when they first joined the service six years earlier and they became fast friends. Kerry was the one person in whom she could confide without it coming back to haunt her.

They exchanged a quick hug.

"I thought you were off today," Kerry said.

"I am. Just getting some practice in." She tipped her head toward the range.

"How was that party the other night?"

"I thought it would be the typical stuffed-shirt event, but if I wasn't on duty I would have had a ball."

"Really?"

"Mmm-hmm." She lowered her voice. "I met Senator Lawson's son, Rafe."

Kerry's green eyes widened. "I've only seen pictures. Is he as gorgeous in person?"

"That would be an understatement." She pushed out a breath. "There's something about him." Her gaze drifted off.

"Did you give him your number?"

"No! Don't be silly. I was on duty."

"So."

"So? I'm not going to lose my job for a turn-on."

"You need a turn-on. When's the last time you got some?"

Avery made a face. "Is that all you can think about?"

"Yes."

They laughed.

"You're a mess."

"Maybe but you still should have given him your number."

"For what? I live in DC and he's in Louisiana."

"Hmm. True. Anyway, what are you doing later?"

"Heading to the gym, then home. Stop by and I'll fix us some mimosas."

"Don't have to ask me twice. I'll bring Chinese from that place we like."

"Sevenish?"

"See you then." Kerry's pager went off. She pulled

it from the clip on her hip and checked the number. "Duty calls."

"Always. And don't forget the extra hot mustard."

"Got it."

They parted and headed in opposite directions.

Maybe she should have given Rafe her number, but now that she thought about it he hadn't asked. Just as well. Relationships were difficult in the best of circumstances. Long distance was worse. Beyond that, her career didn't make for the best in partnerships. At any given time she could be called on to travel halfway across the globe. She'd lost count of how many dinners, getaways and "sleepovers" she'd had to either cancel or end abruptly. Compound that with being the daughter of Horace Richards, the ranking senior senator, and she was never quite sure if a man was with her because of genuine interest or to get close to her father.

Kerry was right, though. It had been a long time since she'd been with a man—in every sense of the word. She did miss being touched, waking up with someone beside her, having doors opened, being told that she was beautiful, having someone to look out for and protect her for a change. *Wishful thinking.*

She got behind the wheel of her Navigator and headed away from headquarters. The imposing images of democracy stood firm against the horizon; the Capitol, the White House and in the distance the Lincoln Memorial. A surge of pride filled her. This was the life she chose—to protect and defend. It was the life she'd been groomed for since college.

Avery spent a full two hours in the gym, part of her weekly regime. She not only worked out to stay fit but for health reasons, as well. Her mother had died of a massive heart attack when Avery was only fifteen. The doctors had warned Linda Richards that if she kept up the fried foods, didn't quit smoking and lose the weight, her outlook was not good. Linda remained stubborn and determined to hold on to her southern-style soul-food cooking, brushing all well-meaning advice aside.

Avery remembered Sunday dinners being more of an extravaganza than a meal. Two kinds of meats—one of which was always fried—collards and string beans seasoned in fatback, six-cheese baked macaroni, sweet tea and pies that would set off diabetic alarms.

Eat up were her mother's two favorite words.

Growing up Avery believed that everyone ate the way her family did, even as she put on the pounds herself. By the time she turned fifteen, shortly before her mother's death, she was 190 pounds at five foot five.

Instead of tears Avery mourned with food, pushing beyond two hundred and ten pounds by her seventeenth birthday. It was her own brush with a health scare that finally turned her around.

It was three months before her high school graduation. For about a week she'd experienced shortness of breath and mild dizzy spells. She wouldn't tell her father. It was bad enough that he looked at her with a mixture of disgust and sadness. The decision was taken out of her hands when she collapsed in the school stairwell.

Two days in the hospital, dependent on an oxygen mask and lectured by doctors, nurses and nutritionists, Avery came home determined to live.

Wrapped in a towel Avery stepped out of a long, hot shower and walked through her two-bedroom condo. It was almost six. Knowing Kerry she would arrive any minute. She had a penchant for turning up early for any and everything. Avery decided on a T-shirt and a pair of shorts.

After getting dressed she put a bottle of wine in the fridge to chill then curled up on the couch to catch up on the news until Kerry arrived.

There was the usual litany of disasters, fires, floods, home invasions and yet another unarmed black man shot by police.

Avery's stomach turned with anguish and disappointment. Anguish for the family and friends and community and disappointment in the profession that she was part of.

As the names of the fallen continued to climb she'd begun to question how the country that she loved had devolved into one of fear of the very people sworn to protect you, and she'd begun to question if in fact she should stay in her line of work.

The newscaster skillfully switched gears to talk entertainment politics. Her heart lurched. There on the screen in bold, living color was Rafe Lawson on the night of his grandfather's birthday party. He was on the small stage in the center of the massive ballroom, playing the sax. Avery leaned in.

"Rafe Lawson, one of Louisiana's most eligible bachelors, and the eldest son and heir to the Lawson legacy is seen here playing a tribute to his grandfather Clive Lawson. The celebration of the 85th birthday of the patriarch was a star-studded affair that included a surprise visit by Vice President Reynolds, a long-time friend to the senior Lawson. His son Senator Branford

Lawson is actively campaigning for the seat of Chairman of the Homeland Security Committee."

Avery couldn't tear her eyes off Rafe and wished that she could hit replay when the station segued to the weather. As if deflated she flopped back against the pillows of the couch. Her pulse continued to race and that funny feeling in the pit of her stomach remained. Crazy that he could have the same effect on her through a television screen as he did up close and personal.

For a moment she closed her eyes and inhaled. His scent awakened in her memory. The sound of his voice, slow, easy and deep, whispered in her ear. A shudder rippled through her and her eyes flew open. She jumped up and went for the wine that was chilling in the fridge. She couldn't wait for Kerry.

She poured a full glass and took a deep swallow. If Kerry hadn't rung the bell when she did, Avery was certain she would have put on her sneakers and ran Rafe Lawson out of her system.

"Hey, girl." Avery stepped aside to let Kerry in. "Hmm, smells good," she said, eyeing the bags in Kerry's hand.

"I am starved." Kerry breezed in and went straight to the kitchen to put down the bags. She moved around Avery's kitchen like it was her own, taking out plates and flatware. "Drinking without me?" she said, noticing Avery's glass of wine. "Thought we were doing mimosas."

"We are. I just needed something to take the edge off."

Kerry stopped emptying the bag of its food cartons. "Why? Something happen?"

"Not exactly." She twisted her lips to the side. "Sort of."

"Okay. I'll bite. What?"

Avery told her about seeing Rafe on television and the crazy way it made her feel.

"Wow. Sounds serious."

"No, it sounds crazy." She opened a carton and loaded her plate with stir-fried vegetables and generously drizzled them with hot mustard.

"So what are you going to do about it?" Kerry crunched on a spring roll.

"Sum it up to a pleasant memory and move on."

Kerry threw her a skeptical glance. "Right."

"I will. You'll see."

Kerry chuckled. "Whatever."

For the most part Avery was as good as her word. In the ensuing weeks she'd all but put images and thoughts of Rafe Lawson in her rearview. Every now and again she had a flash but quickly pushed it back where it belonged. Her tough schedule was a big factor.

Since the night of the party VP Reynolds had been so impressed with her that he'd requested Avery as part of his second-shift detail, which was great for her as it left a good chunk of her day free and occupied some of her evenings. Evenings that would more than likely have been spent alone anyway.

She was at her desk reviewing status reports when she got a call from the lobby security advising her to come down.

"Be right there." She reached into her desk drawer, removed her Glock and slipped it into her underarm holster, then shrugged into her navy blue suit jacket.

Her low-heeled shoes clicked rhythmically against the granite floors. She stopped at the bank of elevators and pressed the down button. Mike walked up and joined her for the wait. Inwardly she groaned and hoped that he wasn't riding all the way down.

"Morning. Heading out?"

"Good morning. No, just to the lobby."

"Listen, Avery..."

The doors swished open.

Avery stepped on and faced forward.

"I'd really like to take you to lunch sometime."

She was so taken aback by the clear tone of sincerity and almost boyish look in his eyes that she couldn't respond. Her lips parted as the doors closed.

Avery shook her head in disbelief and leaned against the back wall of the elevator. That was new and different. Mike had never formally asked her out. He'd always insinuated what a good catch he was, taunted her about her work ethic and goaded her whenever an opportunity presented itself. This was the Mike she'd never met before, but she still didn't trust him.

The doors opened on the main floor. She buttoned her jacket, made certain her ID was visible and walked to the security console.

"Agent Richards. I got a call."

"Yes, Agent Richards. Senator Lawson's son is here to see you."

Her heart felt as if it jumped from her chest to her throat and a hot wave rolled through her from toe to head.

She swallowed. "Thank you." When she turned toward the waiting area, she heard her own gasp when she spotted him. His back was turned to her, but his long, lean form was unmistakable framed within the towering bulletproof windows that looked out onto the nation's capital. The white collar of his shirt peeked above the black jacket that matched his slacks, but when he turned there was not the expected tie, but rather an open collar revealing the tease of hot chocolate. The aura that wafted around him was palpable, even from where she stood.

"Oh, lord," she murmured. She couldn't tell what he saw or what he was thinking behind the dark shades that shielded his eyes, only that his lush lips moved into a slow smile while she approached.

"Mr. Lawson." She stopped in front of him and hoped that he didn't sense her sudden anxiety.

Rafe removed his shades and slid them into the breast pocket of his jacket. Bad move. Now she couldn't think beyond the glow in his eyes and the intoxicating scent of his cologne.

"I hope you don't mind that I looked you up since I was in town."

She had a momentary brain freeze. "Well, I'm not sure if I mind or not. I would guess it depends on why you're here."

That grin again.

"We didn't get a real chance to talk the night of the party." He stepped closer, cutting off the space between them, slid his hands into his pockets and angled his head just a bit to the right. "I thought if I took you to dinner we could pick up where we left off."

Avery blinked rapidly and shifted her weight. "Dinner? I... I really don't think...that would be a good idea."

Rafe gave the barest of shrugs. "Not a problem, only an invitation."

His smile was just enough to stir the imagination.

Avery licked her bottom lip. "So what brings you to DC?"

"Meeting a friend. He's playing a set tonight. Maybe if you're not too busy—not eating dinner—" his eyes cinched with mischief "—you could stop by. You might like it. Good food, adult crowd, great music." He extended his hand.

Avery glanced down and mindlessly placed her hand in his. The shock raced up her arm and raised the hair on the back of her neck. Her fingertips tingled.

Rafe dipped his head toward her. "I'll let you get back to secretly servicing," he said in a wickedly low voice that set her imagination on a chase down the lane of possibility.

"You have a way with words, Mr. Lawson."

Rafe chuckled. "So I've heard." His gaze ran lazily over her then settled on her eyes. "Good to see you again, Agent Richards."

"You…too."

"If you change your mind I'll be at Blues Alley. Set starts at eight, last set at ten."

"I can't promise."

"No promises needed. Enjoy your day."

He turned and strode away and Avery felt he'd taken all the energy with him. She watched him push through the revolving door before merging in with the flow of bodies.

She spun away and right into Mike.

"Friend?"

"What?"

He lifted his chin toward the exit. "Friend of yours? I saw you two talking pretty close. Didn't think you were seeing anyone with you so wrapped up in this job. You really need to think about letting me take you out. Lunch. Dinner."

She was so annoyed that Mike snapped the spell of Rafe that she barely refrained from lathering him with the cuss words that she only held on to by sheer will.

"Excuse me," she said and brushed by him.

Her hand trembled ever so slightly when she pressed the elevator button. She replayed when she'd first met Rafe. They'd barely shared more than a couple of sentences. From what she recalled she'd only given him her first name and certainly no reason for him to believe that he could simply *show up* at her office.

The doors opened. Even more alarming was how he even figured out what her last name was in order to find where she was stationed. *She* was the damned Secret Service! But clearly he must have used his father's connections. She didn't know if she should be flattered or pissed off.

Avery walked down the corridor and back to her small office, and plopped down in the chair behind her desk. Her body still vibrated and her usual methodically organized thoughts were in complete disarray.

She reached for her cell phone and called Kerry. The call went to voice mail, but while she was leaving a message, Kerry called her back.

"Hey, Avery, what's up?"

"You will never guess who just left here."

"Don't make me guess."

"Rafe Lawson," she said in a pressed whisper.

"Say what?"

"Yes! He was here."

"What did he want?"

Avery ran down the conversation.

"So let me get this straight. This fine-ass bachelor flies across the country, takes the time to track you down, asks you out for dinner and you say—no? Are you out of your damned mind?"

"No. I'm...cautious."

"No. Crazy. What do you think can happen over dinner?"

"That's not the point."

"Then what is the point?"

"I don't know," she woefully confessed. She sighed heavily into the phone. "He... There's something about him that...unsettles me."

"What does that even mean?"

"I feel as if I lose control when he's in my space."

"Girl, girl..." Kerry laughed. "I only wish there was someone to make me feel that way."

"I don't. I can't be all foggy-headed and tongue-tied."

"Sis, you have got to give yourself some space to live and be a woman. This job can take a toll on the people in our lives and us. No one knows better than me. But every now and then we have to be our own number one priority."

Avery was quiet. It wasn't that she didn't want to be in a relationship. She just knew at this stage in her life it was almost impossible if she wanted to be successful. She was good at what she did, and after years of trying she'd finally gained, if not the love, at least the admiration of her father. She didn't want to lose that over something that probably would never last.

"I'll make a deal with you," Kerry said, breaking into Avery's thoughts.

"What deal?"

"I'll go with you to Blues Alley and after the evening is over if you still feel the same way...I'll shut my mouth on the subject."

It would give her a chance to see Rafe again without being out there on her own. "Okay."

"Great. So you want to go to the first set or the last?"

"First. I'm on duty tomorrow morning."

"Too bad. I'm off."

"Don't rub it in. Meet you out front at 7:30?"

"Perfect."

"So I'll see you later."

"Later."

Avery disconnected the call and leaned back in her chair. A giddy sensation fluttered in her center. She looked at the time on her phone. Seven hours. This was going to be a very long day.

Chapter 3

It had been several months since he'd been to the DMV area. Driving through the streets of DC brought back a mixture of memories.

He'd partied hard in the nation's capital, frequenting the many clubs and after-hours spots, either as a musician or one of the revelers. He'd been enamored with the city since his youth, enough that he left Tulane's grad school and enrolled in Howard University, much to his father's disappointment, which suited Rafe just fine. The only saving grace was that Branford believed he would be able to keep an eye on his son if he was in the city where he wielded power and also claimed as a second home. Neither reality fazed Rafe in the least. If anything it fueled his bad boy ways: speeding tickets to tabloid news to barroom brawls. Yet somehow he managed to graduate with his master's degree in music history and composition and built a reputation on campus as one of the most talented sax players of his generation. He'd even been offered a teaching position after graduation, but he turned it down. As much as he loved everything about music he wasn't ready to be tied down to one place.

The rows of town houses, in a range of browns and dusty red hues, stood in perfectly proportioned squares of grace, adorned with flower-bearing urns all shaded by century-old trees. The neighborhood was reminiscent of times gone by when the roads were cobblestone and horse-drawn carriages were the preferred mode of transportation.

Rafe parked his rented Mercedes out front and took his carry-on from the trunk. He opened the black gate and walked down the short path to the door. Even though he did not stay in town often, he had Alice come twice per month to clean and air out the rooms. He'd called in advance of this visit to make sure the fridge and the bar were stocked. Alice always did an outstanding job, and as usual today was no exception.

When he walked in he was greeted with a vase of fresh flowers in the foyer and the smell of something delicious coming from the kitchen. He dropped his bag in the hall and followed the scent.

Alice was busy at the sink washing vegetables for a salad. Rafe eased up behind her and slipped his arms around her thick waist.

Alice gave a slight squeal of surprise and giggled like a schoolgirl rather than a grandmother of three when Rafe placed a kiss behind each ear. She playfully smacked his hands.

"Still being a rascal, I see. Half scared me to death."

Rafe kissed her again. "Aw, come on, cher." He turned her around and looked her over. "Still the prettiest girl at the party."

Alice's cheeks flushed. "Oh go on." She shooed him away.

Rafe lifted the cover of the simmering pot and inhaled pure bliss. "Will you marry me, Ms. Alice?" he teased when he saw the jambalaya.

"I have no intention of standing at the end of the line waiting my turn."

"Aww, Ms. Alice, if you promise to fix your famous jambalaya at least once a week, I swear I'll put you right up front."

Alice's round face crinkled with laughter. She wagged a finger at him. "One of these days you're going to run into just the right woman to make an honest man out of you."

"You really think so?" he asked, growing serious.

She looked him in the eye. "If you slow down and stop running so fast you'll see her." She lightly shoved him aside. "Now go on and let me finish up. I'm meeting some friends in town."

"Yes, ma'am."

Rafe retrieved his bag from the hall and went upstairs. His room, like the rest of the house, was as he'd last seen it. But he knew it had been dusted and polished and the linens changed. He went over to the walk-in closet and was pleased to find that his clothes had arrived ahead of him and were neatly hung. He smiled and closed the door. What would he do without Alice?

Rafe slid out of his jacket, tossed it on the club chair by the window then unbuttoned his shirt and let it join his jacket.

A quick shower, a change of clothes and then he needed to get with Quinten about tonight. He was pretty certain that Q would be more than cool with him joining the set tonight, but he didn't want to take anything, especially their friendship, for granted. He wanted to be sure just in case Avery did show up.

He didn't understand why it mattered that she cared or whether she showed up. The very idea that he'd gone through his kid brother to find out who she was, re-arranged his life to fly to DC to see her and was feeling like a horny teen just thinking about her gave him pause.

This was not his MO. Totally out of character. Although he'd been known to be impulsive at times he was always deliberate when it came to the women in and out of his life and the relationships he chose to pursue. In those instances he'd never been driven by emotion but rather need, desire or simply the wish of a woman that he wanted to see satisfied.

Avery. He was uncertain and he didn't particularly like it, but he felt challenged to venture down this new avenue.

Rafe found a parking space a little more than a block from Blues Alley, then took a slow stroll back to the club. As he'd figured when he called Quinten to let him know he was in town, Q was more than happy to have his best friend join him onstage, and Rafe was really looking forward to playing in front of an audience.

He adjusted his sax case over his shoulder and pushed through the doors of the club. He was momen-tarily delayed by an overzealous security guard who advised Rafe that the club didn't open until four, but quickly offered his apologies when Quinten walked over, embraced Rafe in a one-arm hug and introduced him.

"This is my man, Rafe Lawson. He's with the band. Rafe, Phil… He keeps an eye out."

Rafe extended his hand. "Phil."

"My apologies."

"None needed for doing your job."

They shook hands and then Rafe followed Quinten to one of the back rooms.

"How you doing, bruh?" Quinten asked while he pulled open the door to the mini-fridge and took out a bottle of water. He handed it to Rafe and grabbed one for himself. "Glad you called, man."

"Yeah, yeah. Everything's good. Can't complain." He sat on the side of the desk and twisted the top off the water bottle. "It'll be like old times tonight."

"Truth."

"How's Rae?"

"Fine as evah," he said with a grin. "Jamal is in his second year of college. Can you believe that? Tall as me and swears he's all that."

The two friends laughed.

"Chip off the old man's block," Rafe joked. "I'd love to see him."

"Yeah, you need to catch up on your part-time god-father duties."

"Aw man, easy. You got to admit I have never missed a birthday, holiday or graduation."

"Yeah, yeah, you right. Just messing with you."

"Talk to Maxine?" Maxine Sherman and Quinten once had a tumultuous relationship, but Q's heart had been with Nikita. When Nikita died in that car accident,

Rafe wasn't sure if Quinten would ever be right again. Him, their buddy Nick Hunter and his then-girlfriend Parris McKay rallied around Q. Then he met Rae and she literally breathed life back into him. It was well after Nikita's passing that he found out about Jamal—his son with Maxine. Stressful times, but everything worked out. Maxine married Taylor, a great guy who loved Jamal like his own, and Q and Maxine knew that the most important person was their son. When Jamal started high school he came to live with his father and Rae, and then went to Howard.

"Maxine is doing real well. We talk a couple of times a month." He smiled wistfully.

"Ever have any regrets about your relationship with Maxine?"

Quinten gave a shrug. "I used to when J was a kid, but we all made choices and when I met Rae..." he grinned "...that was it. Hooked."

Rafe nodded slowly. "Guess it happens for a chosen few." He pushed up from the side of the desk, took a swallow of water and looked at his friend. "Me? Not happening. I like my life just the way it is, free, easy, no commitments."

"That's what we all say, my brother." He chuckled from deep in his chest and took a band from his pocket to gather up his mid-shoulder-length locs. He fastened them at the nape of his neck. "Come on up front. Let's check the stage and the mics. The rest of the band should be here in a few."

The Quinten Parker Quartet had made a name for themselves touring the States and Europe. Q's wife, Rae, a star in her own right, added a bit of splash to the quartet with her provocative spoken word.

Quinten asked him more times than he could count to join the band. Each time Rafe graciously turned him down. He enjoyed the liberating feeling of playing where and when he wanted, recording in the studio when he was ready, popping up at clubs to be a featured performer, being his own man with his own business. Totally independent. Being tied to anything or anyone didn't work for him. He'd tried it. Once was enough.

"Hey," Quinten said, his tone softened. He anchored his hand on Rafe's shoulder. "It's been a long time." He looked his friend in the eye, knowing.

Rafe's jaw reflexively clenched. "Yeah, it has. Doesn't change anything." His brow arched to punctuate his point.

Quinten held his hands up in submission. "I hear ya." He pushed open the back-room door and they entered the club space.

Rafe stepped up onto the stage. Q was right. It had been a long time, sixteen years and counting. But like he'd said, time didn't change anything. So he filled those years with music, good food, expensive liquor, beautiful women, world travel and trying to forget. That was the life he'd created for himself and he was fine with it.

Chapter 4

Mike fell in step next to Avery as they exited the conference room.

"You never did say who the guy was down at security."

Avery barely glanced at him. "You're right. I didn't." She quickened her pace but Mike matched her stride for stride.

"I'm curious why Senator Lawson's son would be here to see you."

Avery slowed for an instant. Her temper flared, but she would not let Mike get under her skin. "How about it's none of your damned business." She stopped in midstride and spun toward him. "The next time you have the itch to either check the visitor's log or review security footage to check up on me, I'll report you for sexual harassment."

"Whoa! Just hold on. It's nothing like that and you know it."

"Do I?" she challenged. The glint of fire in her eyes held him in place. "Have a good day, Mike, and stay out of my way."

Avery's heart thundered. She hurried down the corridor and back to her office. The weekly staff meeting was draining enough without having to deal with Mike and his nonsense. Something had to change.

She closed her office door behind her, sat at her desk and booted up her computer. She did a quick check of her email, then updated her calendar based on the new assignments given at the meeting. Those minor details out of the way, she checked her service weapon in her underarm holster, took her purse from the bottom drawer and headed out for the day.

Inside her car with her office now in her rearview, she felt herself begin to unwind but quickly felt a different surge of tension as the sound of Rafe's voice came alive in her mind. A mild shudder rippled through her limbs. She gripped the steering wheel tighter.

Seeing him today was simultaneously thrilling and unsettling; thrilling that he went to whatever lengths to find her and unsettling for the very same reason. She was flattered that he sought her out, but the distance that she maintained to protect herself and her space had been breached without her consent.

Clearly Rafe Lawson was the type of man that did what he wanted whenever he desired and he had the money, the connections and the charisma to pull it all off.

Avery parked in the garage and entered the two-bedroom Tudor through the kitchen. Her cell phone vibrated in her purse.

"I'm just walking in the door," Avery said, catching Kerry's call before it went to voice mail.

"Just checking to make sure you didn't chicken out."

"Very funny. Why would I do that?" She tugged open the double-door stainless steel fridge and took out a bottle of water.

"Because I know you, that's why. Anyway, what are you wearing?"

"To be honest I hadn't really thought about it." She took a long replenishing swallow.

"Hmm. Well, I'm going casual. My white crepe slacks and that magenta blouse that I got from the mall and those strappy white Michael Kors sandals…some accessories. Yeah, that's what I'll wear."

Avery shook her head and smiled. Kerry's idea of casual was runway ready. "Sounds perfect. Guess I better get moving and find something appropriate so that I won't look like the poor relation," she said over her laughter.

"Girl, please, you couldn't look bad coming out of a street fight. Why do you think I always have to step up my game when we go out?"

"K, please," she sniffed and finished off her water.

"I'm serious. You are so focused on your job and scoping out bad guys that you are totally oblivious to the effect you have. Rafe Lawson tracking your behind down is a perfect example. Do you have any idea who he really is?"

Avery started toward her bedroom. "Yes. He's Senator Lawson's son. He's wealthy and well connected."

"You are pitiful. Girl, Google him. He's a lot more

than a wealthy senator's son. I'll meet you out front of the club at 7:30."

"Fine. See you later." She tossed her phone on the bed. Kerry always made everything more dramatic than it really was. She should have gone into acting instead of law enforcement.

Avery opened her closet door and stood staring at her rather ordinary line-up of outfits, the majority of which were navy and gray skirt and slack suits. She had one formal dress that she'd worn to the Lawson party and her go-to jersey wrap dress in a deep navy blue. She took the navy dress from the rack and laid it out on the bed then went to hop in the shower.

Avery's hands shook ever so slightly as she put silver hoops in her ears. Nervous. What did she have to be jittery about? She was going to a jazz club with her best friend, something she'd done hundreds of times. But none of those times had Rafe Lawson invited her.

Her heart beat faster. She drew in a long, deep breath and briefly shut her eyes. Just another night out, she told herself. She took her purse from the dresser, dropped her wallet, keys and phone inside and headed out.

It took a bit of time to find parking. The lot behind Blues Alley was full and street parking was at a premium. Avery finally found a spot two blocks off Constitution Avenue. The short walk back gave her a chance to put on her game face and settle the flare-up of nerves.

As she approached the club she spotted Kerry standing outside with her focus on her cell phone. She glanced up and smiled when she saw Avery.

"Hey."

"Hi. You weren't waiting long, were you?"

"No, just got here," Kerry said.

"Parking is crazy."

"I know, I think I got the last spot in the lot."

"Lucky."

They both turned toward the entrance and went inside. It had been a while since she'd been to Blues Alley. The last act she'd seen perform was a special appearance by Wynton Marsalis.

"Good evening, ladies. Do you have a reservation?" the hostess asked.

"No. We don't," Kerry said.

"It might be a bit of a wait for a table."

Avery and Kerry took a quick look around. The club was full.

"Busy night," Avery commented.

"Quinten Parker always draws a crowd. I can get you a setup at the bar until a table opens."

The friends took a quick glance at each other and nodded in unified agreement.

"Right this way." The hostess led them over to the bar and took their names for the waiting list.

"Didn't think about making reservations for a weeknight," Kerry said as she hopped up on the bar stool. "The band is really good."

"I think I have one of his early CDs," Avery said. She placed her purse on her lap and looked around.

"You see him?" Kerry asked knowingly.

Avery adjusted her bottom on the stool. "No." She linked her fingers together and worked at being unconcerned. But that didn't stop her pulse from jackhammering in her veins.

"What can I get you, ladies?" The bartender wiped the spaces in front of them with a damp cloth.

"Apple martini," Avery said.

"Make that two," Kerry added.

"Coming right up." He placed a bowl of mixed nuts and one of taco chips with dip in front of them.

Rafe walked out front from the greenroom along with Quinten to check the crowd.

"You definitely can bring them in," Rafe said, congratulating Quinten with a pat on the back.

"Blues Alley is my second home when I leave New York."

"Haven't been to New York for a minute," Rafe said. He leaned against the frame of the archway. "Need to get this next album finished."

"How much more to go?"

"At least three more tracks to lay down."

"Your last one was off the chain, man." They bumped fists. "Anytime you want to come up to Harlem I have some of the best engineers in the business. Pure genius. And the next project we need to do together."

Rafe slowly nodded in agreement. "Yeah. For sure." He turned his head and when a waitress moved he spotted Avery at the bar. "Be right back." He started off before Quinten could respond.

Rafe glided between tables and around bodies blocking his pathway to the bar. He eased behind her.

"Glad you could make it," he whispered against her neck.

Avery felt her entire body tingle. She angled toward him as he came up beside her.

"Rafe," she managed to say and was caught up for a moment in the light of his eyes.

Kerry turned.

Avery cleared her throat. "Rafe Lawson, this is my friend Kerry Holt. Kerry, Rafe Lawson."

"Pleasure." He gave Kerry a gallant nod and a smile. "I have a table," he said to them both, but his focus was on Avery. "You're more than welcome, unless you prefer the bar."

"Absolutely not," Kerry answered for them both. She stuck a twenty under the bowl of nuts to cover both their drinks, then slid down off her bar stool.

Avery wanted to elbow Kerry but restrained herself. "Thanks. They didn't say how long the wait for a table would be."

"My pleasure." He placed his hand on her lower back as she got off the stool.

"Right this way."

Avery used all of her concentration to put one foot in front of the other to avoid succumbing to the heat of his large hand right above the rise of her rear.

"It's the one in the center, up front," he said close to her ear and she knew it was that thing he did to get close to her and it worked—again.

They stopped at the table and Rafe helped them both into their seats. "Can I get you ladies anything?"

"We're good for now," Avery said, and held up her half-finished drink.

Rafe nodded. "Totally understand. But when you get hungry they have a great menu and it's on the house."

"Oh, you don't have to—"

Kerry cut her off. "Thank you. That's very generous."

Rafe took a step back. "Enjoy your evening, ladies. See you later?" he stated to Avery in a mouthed whisper.

Avery didn't respond as she watched him stroll away.

"Oh. My. God," Kerry whispered and fanned herself with the menu. She leaned forward and stared Avery in the eyes. "Listen here, girl, if you don't know what you want to do with all that—I'll handle it for you."

"He…is…something," she admitted.

"That's putting it mildly and he is so charming."

They laughed and for a moment Avery allowed herself to imagine "what if."

Kerry raised her glass and shifted Avery's focus.

"What are we toasting?" Avery asked.

"To possibility." She grinned.

Avery twisted her lips. "To possibility."

"Now let's order our on-the-house dinner, 'cause I'm starved."

"Did you research him like I told you?" Kerry asked while she sliced through her medium-well steak.

"No. Didn't have time."

Kerry stopped cutting and reached for her purse on the empty chair. She rifled through and pulled out an inch-thick stack of papers clipped together. "That's what I figured." Kerry placed the papers next to Avery's plate. "So I did it for you."

Avery gave her the side-eye.

"I know. Don't thank me now." Kerry proceeded to dig into her steak.

"Kerry," she said in a hot whisper. "I don't believe you did this."

Kerry wagged her fork at Avery. "Let me just say this…" She leaned closer. "That man is a serious catch.

Money, looks, connections, well-traveled, educated, talented and other than some minor brushes with the law over a motorcycle accident a couple of years back, he is damn near too good to be true."

"Then why isn't he with someone or married if he's all that?" Avery countered, still unwilling to take the bait. "Must be something wrong."

"According to the articles he's been linked to dozens of women, from socialites to supermodels, and none of them have a bad word to say about him." She shrugged. "Maybe he's looking for you." She giggled and winked.

"Sure. Right." But she couldn't help wonder why he was single and what if Kerry was right? Now she was being silly. Clearly Rafe Lawson had mastered the art of being a playboy. It was as simple as that.

"Good evening, ladies and gentlemen. Welcome to Blues Alley. We have a very special lineup tonight. He may live in New York but he can call DC home anytime—Quinten Parker and the Quartet."

The room erupted into applause. "That's not all. Bringing his own brand of Louisiana jazz is Mr. Saxophone himself, Rafe Lawson."

Kerry's eyes widened with delight. Avery's lips parted in disbelief.

"Did you know?" Kerry whispered.

"No. I had no idea. He told me his friend was playing a set."

"You do know that among all of his other fineness, he is an amazing sax player with music awards for his albums. Girl, get with the program." Kerry joined the rest of the audience in applauding the band as they took the stage.

Avery mindlessly joined in and made up her mind that she would actually read up on Rafe Lawson.

Incredible was the only word to describe the first set. Avery remained enthralled with every note, every shift in tempo, and there were no words to explain the rush of sensations that flowed through her whenever Rafe stepped into the spotlight, his long, lean form bent and curved with each note, and transported them with his version of Coltrane classics, the quartets' numbers and his own originals.

He made love to his audience each time his lips touched the reed and Avery couldn't even imagine what the real thing would be like.

The room erupted and many of the enthused guests rose to their feet as the members of the band took their bows.

Kerry slapped her palms on the table. "Girl...that was some playing!"

"I know that's right," Avery agreed. She slowly shook her head from side to side as the remnants of the experience flowed through her.

Kerry leaned closer. "I'm at a loss as to what to say about your Mr. Lawson. That's pure sex that floats around him like an aura. I swear I thought that woman in the red dress was going to throw herself or her panties onstage if he hit another high note."

They burst out laughing.

"Made a complete fool of herself," Avery said over her chuckles even as she felt the same way the woman did.

"Here he comes," Kerry said from between her teeth.

"Mind if I sit?" Rafe asked and looked from one to the other, but his gaze returned to Avery.

"Of course. Please," Kerry said, saving Avery from looking like a fool or simply plain rude.

"Thanks." He pulled out a chair and sat. "How was dinner?"

"Delicious," Avery managed to say.

Rafe stroked his smooth chin. "How'd you like the set?"

Avery smiled and grew hot inside. "Loved it. You're really amazing."

His deep eyes crinkled at the corners, the dark orbs fanned by thick lashes. He placed the barest tip of his finger on her knuckle and a shot of electricity lifted the hairs on the back of her neck. He leaned in. "Gonna hang around for the second set?"

He was so close she could see her reflection in his eyes, the tiny scar just above his right brow and the perfect curve of his mouth. She had no plans to stay and for the life of her she could not explain even under oath why she said yes.

"Did you drive?"

"Um, yes."

He pushed back from the table and stood. "See you shortly." He turned and walked away.

Avery finally breathed.

"My eyelashes are singed from all of the sparks flying."

Avery made a face. She rested her elbows on the table and propped her chin on her palm.

"He asked if I drove," she said, her voice low.

Kerry's eyes widened. "Hmm. I think that's my cue."

"What are you talking about?"

"I'm saying that he is looking for some personal time that does not include a third party."

"Don't be silly."

"I'm being real. He wants to spend some time with you, not us," she added wagging her finger between the two of them.

Avery's gaze followed the spotlight as the band came back onstage. When Rafe took his place, she realized that she wanted that time together, too.

By the time the set was finished, Kerry had said her goodbyes and made Avery swear that she wouldn't leave out any details.

Avery didn't know what details there would be to tell, but she promised anyway. In the meantime all she could do was keep her imagination from running out of control.

Chapter 5

"Where'd you park?" Rafe asked as he guided Avery out of the front door and into the cool evening.

"Two blocks down," she said, pointing in the direction of her car.

"I'll walk you."

She was going to protest but knew instantly that she wouldn't mean it.

They fell into step together and Rafe confidently placed his arm lightly around her waist and adjusted his sax case on his opposite shoulder.

"I'm really glad you came tonight. I hope it was worth it."

Avery took a quick glance at him. "So am I," she admitted. "And it was."

He hummed in his throat.

"Thanks for introducing me to Quinten. He is so laid-back."

Rafe chuckled. "Yes. Mr. Chill himself. Sorry you didn't get to meet his wife, Rae. Totally amazing sister. Maybe next time."

"Maybe…"

The tips of his fingers pressed a little against her side. "Looking forward."

"This is me," she said and came to a stop in front of her car.

Rafe released her and she dug in her purse for her keys.

"Let me get that for you." He took the keys from her, opened the door and helped her in before handing them back.

"Thank you."

"How far are you from here?"

"Dupont Circle."

"I'll follow you. Make sure you get home safely."

"You really don't have to do that."

"Yes, I do. Wait here. I'm going to get my car."

Before she could protest further he'd turned and headed back to the club. Her thoughts ran all over the place. She certainly hoped that he didn't think she was going to invite him in. She wanted to but she would never… What if she did let him in? No, that would send the wrong message. But it would be rude not to, wouldn't it?

While her thoughts were on autopilot, a car horn honked. She glanced out of her window. Rafe pulled up alongside her. His window lowered.

"I'll follow you."

"Uh, okay." She pulled herself together enough to start her car and ease out without hitting anything.

The ten-minute drive was the most nerve-wracking

experience of her life. It took all of her wits to stay focused on the road and not her rearview mirror. She was so consumed with tension that she almost missed the turn onto her street.

When she finally pulled into her driveway relief couldn't describe how she felt. She jumped at the tapping on her window. She lowered the window.

"Are you okay?"

"Yes. Fine." She smiled.

"Going in?" he asked, with what sounded like amusement in his voice.

"Of course." She took her purse from the passenger seat, extracted the key from the ignition and accepted his hand.

When she was drawn to her feet, mere inches separated them. Her gaze landed on his collarbone and she realized how tall he actually was and how his lean frame belied the power beneath.

Avery swallowed and stepped around him. Her heart banged mercilessly as she walked to her front door with Rafe a half step behind.

She turned. "Thanks so much for inviting me tonight. I had a great time."

His eyes picked up the light from the moon and seemed to sparkle. He grinned, leaned down and placed a featherlight kiss on her forehead. "Good night. Rest well. I hope you don't mind if I call on you again."

"You're going to fly all the way from Louisiana to DC just to see me?"

"My family has a place in Arlington, Virginia. When I have good reason, I stay there." He leveled his gaze on her. "Do I have good reason?"

"You might," she managed to say.

That grin again.

Rafe lifted his chin toward the door. "Want to make sure you get in safely."

Avery ran her keys through her fingers, turned and somehow managed to get the key in the lock. She opened the door and flipped on the light in the foyer. She faced him. "See? Safe and sound. Thanks...again."

"My pleasure, cher." He took a step back, turned and strode to his car.

Avery waited a beat before closing the door. She stood frozen in place while she listened to the rev of his engine. She took a quick peek between the slats of the blinds. Only her car remained.

Rafe pulled into his driveway, killed the engine and slid out. When he walked into the house he sniffed the air and smiled.

Alice had fixed her should-be-world-famous peach cobbler. The sweet syrupy aroma sprinkled with cinnamon still hung in the air. His mouth watered but it was a little too late to indulge.

He bypassed the kitchen. What he could use, however, was a shot of bourbon. He crossed into the den, went to the bar and fixed his drink. He took a deep swallow and closed his eyes as the warmth of the rich amber brew slid down his throat and settled in his belly before exploding into a burst of heat that slowly coursed through his veins.

He took his drink and went to the lounge chair and sat. Absently he rotated the glass on the end table as he relived the evening. Whenever he played he allowed the music to transport him, lift him, fill him. Often he would forget he was on a stage and in front of an audience and simply succumb to the notes, become one with them. Tonight was no exception, but he also played for Avery. When his fingers ran up and down the sax, it was her body that he imagined. When he blew soft, high, low into his reed it was her skin that he whispered against. For him, the making of music was akin to making love. It was an art, one to be nurtured, explored, experienced and shared. But tonight...

He took another sip of his drink. Tonight was a whole other level. He set his glass down and stood. *Avery Richards*. If he allowed it she could get under his skin. She might see things that he didn't want seen. He wasn't up for that.

He took a long cool shower and turned in for the night. Tomorrow he would head home.

Avery couldn't sleep. She kept replaying the moments that she and Rafe stood on the front steps, when he leaned down and kissed her. She touched her forehead. He may as well have branded her. She still felt out of body; unable to control her thoughts or the sudden vibrations that bolted through her without warning.

The printouts that Kerry had given her were spread out on the bed and on her lap. Kerry was right. Rafe Lawson was everything she'd said and then some. More than being the heir to the Lawson fortune and all the tropes that came with it, he was his own man. There were articles that chronicled his world travels, his education, the women he'd dated, his celebrated music, his run-in with the law, his philanthropy, and the rumors of the rift between him and his powerful father. In one interview he said that he had no intention of following in the path of his father. Politics, he'd said, were for those that craved power and it had the potential to change anyone, even those with the best of intentions, and he had no intention of changing.

What the articles couldn't capture was his persona, the raw magnetism that ensnared you, the eyes that held you, the rugged voice with a hint of southern flavor that caressed you, or the way his touch set off shock waves in your body.

Avery shook her head, sighed and gathered up the papers, then stuck them in her nightstand. She got up and went to the shower with the hope of slowing her racing thoughts.

No sooner was she out of the shower when her cell phone chirped. She crossed the room to her nightstand and snatched up the shimmying phone. She smiled and shook her head.

"Do you know it's late?"

"So what. I couldn't wait until tomorrow. And unless you're in the middle of a 'sleepover...'"

Avery feigned a huff. "Fiiine," she conceded and flopped down on her bed. She crossed her ankles. "Well, after you abandoned me..." She went on to give Kerry a blow-by-blow, up to and including the kiss on the forehead.

"What! You let him leave?"

"What was I supposed to do, force him to stay?"

"Yes!"

Avery burst out laughing. "Girl, you are crazy."

"Say what you want but if it hadda been me... I'm just saying."

"Look, I'm tired. I have to be in the office in the morning."

"Fine. Did he at least promise to call?"

"Yes."

"That's a start. Home or work?"

Avery paused a beat. She'd never given him her cell. The only way to reach her was at the office. "Cell," she said, detesting that she lied to her best friend, but hating more that she would have to admit that he actually never asked for her number.

"Well, get some rest. It's house-cleaning day for me tomorrow. So when I take a break I'll give you a call."

"Sounds good. Chat then."

"Night."

"Night."

Avery absently placed the phone on the nightstand. Rafe said he would call. Clearly it was a line—one that he probably used on a regular basis.

She slid between the sheets and switched off the bedside light. No reason to feel a tickle of disappointment. She turned on her side. She wasn't looking for the night out to be any more than what it was. She got what she expected and nothing more.

Rafe Lawson. He was her last thought before she was finally able to drift off to sleep.

Avery was running late and in an irritable mood on top of that. It had taken her much too long to finally fall asleep and then she'd slept through her alarm. She couldn't find a pair of stockings, so she'd had to change out of her dress into slacks and a jacket. To top that off it was raining buckets.

When it rained in DC, drivers acted as if they'd never been behind the wheel of a car. Traffic inched along the road like beginning skaters at the ice rink. By the time she arrived at her office she was one knot of annoyance and the last person she wanted to deal with was Mike.

"Rough night?" he greeted her as he stepped onto the elevator with her.

She swiveled her head in his direction a la horror movie and pinned him in place with a hard stare.

"Not today, Mike. I'm not in the mood."

"Sorry to hear that." He slid his hands into his pockets. "Can I get you some coffee? Always makes me feel better."

She glanced at him and was surprised to find what looked like sincerity in his eyes. Her expression softened. "Thanks. That might help." She offered a tired smile.

The doors slid open.

"Light and sweet?"

"Yes. Thanks."

They parted; he headed to the staff lounge and she to her office.

The message light on her desk phone flashed. She groaned. It was barely nine.

She shrugged out of her jacket, slipped it onto the back of her chair and stabbed the flashing light. Her father's distinct raspy voice filled the room and ruffled her stomach.

"I would have expected you to be at your desk. I'm free for lunch and I'd like you to join me at the Capitol. I'll order for us both. One o'clock. See you then."

Avery shut her eyes and sucked in a long breath. No preamble pleasantries when it came to Horace Richards. Never or rarely a "How are you," just blunt, to the point, as if anything beyond that was a waste of his time. It would never occur to her father that his only daughter might have plans of her own. Even if she did, it wouldn't matter to him. He would expect that she would cancel her plans.

The light tap on the door turned her away from her smoldering thoughts. Mike stuck his head in.

"Coffee is served."

As much as she didn't want to, she smiled. "Thanks."

He walked in and set the cup on her desk.

Avery wrapped her fingers around the paper cup and brought it to her lips. She took a short sip and hummed in appreciation.

"Are you sure everything is okay?"

She glanced up at him. "Yes, I'm fine. Really. And thanks for the coffee." She lifted the cup.

Mike nodded, turned and walked out.

Avery leaned her head back against the headrest of her high-back chair. She was much more comfortable with Mike "the adversary," the pain in the ass, not Mike the actual nice guy.

Her office phone rang.

"Agent Richards."

"Good morning, cher."

Her pulse jumped. "Rafe…good morning."

"I decided to stay in town one more night."

"Oh…"

"If you're free I'd like to take you to dinner."

"Dinner… All right."

"Eight?"

"Eight sounds fine."

"Here's my number…in case you ever need me."

Her hand shook as she tapped the numbers into her cell phone contact list.

"Should I call when I'm on my way?"

Avery grinned. "No need. I'll be ready, but that's my number—just in case."

"I'll commit it to memory. Enjoy your day, now," he said in that down easy way of his.

"You, too."

Avery hung up the phone and felt as if she could levitate out of her chair. That crazy, giddy sensation ran through her limbs and she had the overwhelming urge to do the happy dance, and then she noticed the flashing message light. She pressed the red light and her mood shifted from great to ecstatic. Her father had to cancel lunch. Avery grinned in delighted relief. Her day was getting better by the minute.

Avery had brought Kerry up to speed on everything from Mike's coffee run to her father's cancellation and of course, Rafe's offer of dinner.

"You have got to get something to wear," Kerry insisted as they stepped outside of the café following their "emergency girl lunch."

The midafternoon was springtime warm, perhaps more so than for this time in May. The DC streets teemed with lunch-goers and strollers taking in the unseasonably warm weather. They walked around a family that stopped in the middle of the sidewalk to take pictures.

"Actually, I agree with you, but I don't have time."

Kerry hooked her arm through Avery's. "We'll make time. I know this great boutique and you'll find something to love. Promise. Let's go."

Less than an hour later Avery was back in her office with a deep teal–colored dress in some kind of cotton blend that clung to her body in all the right places. The sleeveless dress had a loose dropping neckline that only hinted at the treasures below. The dress stopped just above the knee and Kerry insisted on a gloss for her legs in lieu of stockings. And what was a brand-new dress that oozed sex and sophistication without the perfect accessories? She purchased teardrop earrings and a thin silver chain for her neck. Avery took one last look at the dress, zipped up the garment bag and hung it up on the coatrack, then tucked her shopping bag of goodies in her desk drawer.

She had a detail assignment that shouldn't take more than two hours. She was to accompany the Speaker of the House to a news conference in the rotunda. For the last six months her assignments had been stateside. She was getting itchy for something more challenging. Normally she was slated for international detail.

When she'd entered the Secret Service most of her assignments had been abroad since she spoke fluent French, Italian, Spanish and had a healthy command of Mandarin. All the language courses she took in high school and through college paid off. But recently she didn't have much chance to use them and she didn't want to get rusty. She made a mental note to speak to her supervisor about considering her for the next out-of-country assignment. Although she'd been assigned to the VP, his schedule for the next month was all within the States.

She checked her weapon in her shoulder holster and the reserve strapped to her ankle, then headed out to the Speaker's office to provide his escort to the conference. Although it was beyond rare that any type of threat or attack transpired in the Capitol rotunda, every precaution was always taken. At least being on guard, listening to speeches and the babble of reporter questions would keep her mind off the night ahead.

Chapter 6

It had been a while since Rafe had made dinner reservations in DC, but it was clear by the deference shown to him when he called Le Galleria that the Lawson name carried plenty of weight in the "chocolate city."

Initially he'd been told that the restaurant was booked. He'd started to simply say thanks and hang up, but then he was asked to leave his name in the event of a cancellation. All he said was Lawson and the conversation immediately shifted.

"Senator Lawson! Why didn't you say so? I'm so sorry. Of course we can find—"

"Thank you, but this is not the senator. This is his son Rafe Lawson. I'm only in town for the evening."

"Of course, of course. Excellent, sir."

Rafe could almost see the harried maître d' scrambling to find the best table.

"We actually have the chef's table available at 8:30. I know you will be pleased."

"I'm sure. Thank you."

"When you arrive please ask for me, Paul Benoit. I'll take care of you and your guest personally."

"I'll do that." He disconnected the call and shook his head, bemused. He'd never been one to cash in on the family name. If anything he made a point of distancing himself. But…sometimes…

Absently, he tossed the phone onto the bed, stripped out of his clothes and changed into sweats. A quick workout in the gym was what he needed.

He grabbed a bottle of water from the fridge, then walked to the back of the house to one of the spare rooms that he'd converted into a personal gym, complete with state-of-the-art equipment.

He started with the treadmill that boasted a video screen programmed to broadcast anything from running in place to navigating a major city marathon. He set the speed and incline to a challenging level, then selected running through the woods. After thirty minutes he switched off to some weight training.

Physical stimulation always helped to clear his head and burn off the excess noise. Lately, he'd been more keyed up than usual. Playing music didn't really help, riding his motorcycle at breakneck speeds wasn't the answer, even his religious workouts couldn't seem to stem the tide of restlessness that continued to rush to the surface lately.

He stood beneath the hot, pounding water of the shower, rolled his neck and shoulders. Usually this unwanted feeling was short-lived. He'd force it out of his system. But recently—the past couple of months at least—he'd been in this land of limbo, simply going through the motions. It wasn't something he could put words to or that he talked about, even to Quinten or his brother Justin. He'd get through it, he always did.

Rafe turned off the shower and stepped out. A night with a woman who definitely intrigued him might fill in the blanks—at least for a while.

Avery by nature was not a pacer, but she found herself pacing back and forth across her bedroom floor. Rather than having just enough time to get showered and dressed, she had too much time and now had to tick off the minutes until Rafe arrived.

He'd sent a text earlier to let her know that the reservations were for 8:30 and he would be there to pick her up about 7:45. It was only 7:30 and the fifteen minutes felt like an eternity.

She checked her purse to ensure that she had her keys and wallet. Checked her riot of curls pulled up and away from her face, her makeup, her teeth, turned left, right and center in front of the mirror until there was nothing left to do. Just when she knew she would self-combust from anticipation the doorbell rang.

Her heart hammered. She drew in a breath, lifted her chin and walked out of her bedroom to the door. She paused for a moment then turned the knob.

He stood facing her when she pulled the door open and when he slowly caressed her with that easy smile that started at the right corner of his mouth, and pinned her in place with the hint of something alluring in his eyes, it took all she had not to gasp.

"Hi," she managed to say.

"Evening." His gaze took her in from top to bottom

in a heated sweep. The darkness in his eyes lit in admiration. "Lovely."

Her cheeks heated. "Thank you. Come in. Please." She stepped aside to let him pass and her eyes momentarily fluttered closed when she caught a hint of his scent.

Avery shut the door. "Can I get you anything before we leave?" she asked in an attempt to wrestle her thoughts under control.

He moved slowly and deliberately toward her the way a panther moves in on his prey. Instinct told her to flee but she couldn't move.

Rafe stepped into her space, cupped her cheek in his palm then lowered his mouth to hers. The air ceased to move, even as currents of electrifying jolts zipped through her veins.

He moved his mouth over hers until her lips parted and his tongue teased hers. Her head spun.

Rafe stepped back but he didn't remove his hand from her cheek. "I'll wait here," was all he said.

It took a moment for Avery to process what happened following his casual comment.

"Be right back," she said just above a whisper. She hurried off toward her bedroom and for an instant was terrified that he might follow her. Then what? She muttered a curse and pushed open her bedroom door.

Avery paused for a moment in front of her mirror. Her copper complexion was heightened by a telltale tinge of red undertone. She raised her hand to the cheek that Rafe held. It was hot as if she'd sat too long near a flame or out in the sun. She ran her tongue across her bottom lip. Just a hint of his taste, only enough to tease. Drawing in a long breath, she took her purse from on top of the dresser and her multicolor open-front caftan from the hanger. It was longer in the back and shorter in the front with hot splashes of teal that matched her dress. She slid her arms through the wide sleeves and went back to meet her date, her regalness flowing and floating around her.

Rafe glanced up from examining a small African sculpture on the coffee table. His eyes caught the light and that slow smile illuminated the space around him.

"Gorgeous." He crossed the room to where she stood framed in the archway.

Avery thought he was going to kiss her again. She was prepared this time but also disappointed when instead he took her hand.

"Ready?"

"Yes, I believe I am." She pushed conviction that she did not feel into her voice.

He held on to her hand as they walked to the front door, opened it for her then took the keys from her hand and locked up behind them.

With the barest of pressure from the tips of his fingers at the lowest part of her back, he guided her to the passenger side of the Mercedes-Benz coupe.

Every move he made was sensual, sexually charged, yet it was as natural to him as breathing.

Avery slid into the plush leather seat and focused on settling her racing heart. Her body thrummed like a plucked tuning fork and Rafe Lawson knew exactly how to play it.

He got in next to her, turned the key in the ignition and the seat belts locked in place.

Rafe gave her a quick look. "All set?"

"Yep." She linked her fingers together on her lap.

"Music?"

"Sure."

He pressed a button on the console and the space filled with a jazz instrumental by an artist she could not name but totally enjoyed.

"So…how did your Secret Servicing go today? Catch any bad guys?"

Avery bit back a smile. How he managed to take a job title and make it sound trashy and sexy at the same time tickled her.

"My Secret Servicing was just fine, thank you very much. The usual high-drama excitement of standing around looking threatening without appearing to be there at all."

"That's a skill, I'm sure," he said over low rumbles of laughter.

She snatched a look at him and saw the crinkle of merriment around his dark eyes. She shook her head, bemused and pleasantly relaxed. The knot that her body had been in unraveled. Her racing heart slowed to its normal rhythm. She felt good. Rafe simply had a knack for smoothing all the edges without appearing to try.

"What about you?"

He lifted his chin and tilted his head to the side. "Hmm, you mean after I spent all day thinking of to-night?"

Avery smiled. "Okay, yeah, after that."

"Took care of a few business calls, worked on some music, spent a couple of hours in the gym, made reservations, took a long, hot shower…and here I am." He lifted his hands for a moment from the steering wheel, turned to her and winked.

For a hot second she imagined him all wet and naked. She swallowed and had to briefly look away.

"It's been a while since I've been to DC for a night out. Where do you usually go?"

Avery drew in a short breath. "Hmm, I wish I could tell you. It's been a while."

"Why? Job?"

"Mostly."

"So…if it's not *all* the fault of the job…"

Avery lowered her gaze. "It's not that I don't go out…*ever*…just that it's few and far between. My choice," she quickly added. "You, on the other hand," she said, eager to turn the light off on her, "are a regular club goer."

"Don't believe everything you read, darlin'." He gave her a quick look.

"I always try to see beyond the obvious."

"Is that right? And what do you see?"

Her heart thumped. "I'm still looking," she said softly.

Rafe pulled to the curb and parked. He angled his body toward her. "Then I'm gonna have to make sure you find what you're looking for. Won't I?" That slow grin eased across his mouth. He opened his door and got out.

Avery bit down on her bottom lip. *Lawd, help me.*

Chapter 7

Le Galleria, known for its upscale clientele, clearly lived up to its reputation. There was an air of subdued classiness, from the décor, plush secluded seating and mood lighting to the rippling murmurs of the DC elite.

Rafe held lightly on to Avery's waist as he led her toward the hostess podium.

"Reservation?" the young woman asked.

"Two for Lawson."

Her brows rose a fraction and the practiced smile went on full display. "Yes, Mr. Lawson. Mr. Benoit wanted to be informed when you arrived. Please wait one moment while I call for him."

Rafe turned to Avery and gave a nonchalant shrug at her inquiring expression. He stepped closer to her so that her hip brushed against his thigh.

"What's that about?" she mouthed.

"Nothing, darlin'. Mr. Benoit and I spoke earlier and he wanted to say hello when we got here is all."

Avery studied him for a moment and caught the glint of mirth in his eyes and knew there was more to the story, but she wouldn't press.

"Mr. Lawson." A man about five foot five with snow-white hair and the demeanor and bearing of an aristocrat hurried up to them and stopped in front of Rafe. He extended his pale, well-manicured hand. "So very glad that you could make it." He turned cool gray eyes on Avery, clasped her hand and dry-kissed her knuckles. "Madam, welcome to Le Galleria."

Avery did all she could to keep from giggling. She smiled politely instead.

"Please come this way. Your table is ready."

Rafe once again slid his arm around Avery's waist as they fell in step behind Mr. Benoit.

They were escorted to the rear of the restaurant to a private seating area where a waiter and the chef were already in place.

"This is our head chef, Chef Fontaine. He will personally prepare your meal."

"Welcome to Le Galleria. Whatever you wish for tonight will be my pleasure to prepare," Chef Fontaine said with a flourish.

Rafe nodded in acknowledgment.

"And this is Spencer. He will be your server tonight," Mr. Benoit intoned.

Spencer gave a slight bow before pulling out the chair for Avery.

"Thank you," she said, glancing up and over her shoulder.

"Your drinks tonight are on the house," Mr. Benoit added. "Enjoy your evening."

Rafe nodded and sat down as Benoit spun away followed by Chef Fontaine.

Spencer placed drink menus in front of them. "Do you need a few moments?"

"I know what I'm having." He glanced across at Avery through lowered lids. "What about you, darlin'?"

"I know what I'm having, as well," she tossed back, well aware of the double entendre, and tingled inside when Rafe's gaze fell on her in full effect.

The corner of his mouth lifted just a bit. "Ladies first."

Avery ran her tongue lightly across her lips. "Apple martini."

"For you, sir?"

"Bourbon on the rocks."

Spencer filled both of their glasses with sparkling water from the carafe before he eased away. "Would you care for appetizers while you decide on your meal?"

"Oysters Rockefeller for starters," Rafe said.

"Right away."

Rafe turned his full attention on Avery. "Do you like oysters? I should have asked."

Avery smiled. "Love them."

He raised his glass of sparkling water. "To an evening of new beginnings and a meeting of the minds."

She tapped her glass against his.

"Hope you don't mind all the extra attention." He sipped his water.

She smiled coyly. "On-the-job hazard. I watch from a discreet distance. Although on those rare occasions when I'd be out to dinner with my father, lobbyists would fall all over themselves to get my father's attention."

"The story of my life." He leaned forward and rested his forearms on the white linen-covered table.

"Does it bother you that much?"

"What? The attention?"

"Carrying around the Lawson name."

Rafe tugged in a long breath. "And there you have the reason."

Avery tilted her head slightly to the side. "I know the feeling or should I say *don't* know the feeling." She focused on her glass of water.

"Meaning?"

She was thoughtful for a moment then looked him in the eye. "My father is fueled by the adulation and the power that comes with his position. It's all that ever seemed to matter to him."

Rafe caught the barest hitch in her voice and the way her eyes dimmed. "And you wanted his attention."

Her brows flicked. "Yes, I did."

Spencer returned with their drinks and appetizer. "Are you ready to order?" He looked from one to the other.

Rafe flipped open his menu. Avery did the same.

"I'll have the steak medium well and the house salad," Avery said.

"Make that two. Please."

"Right away," Spencer said.

Rafe turned his attention to Avery. He wrapped his long fingers around his glass. "Sisters or brothers?"

"No. Only child. I guess I have that syndrome."

Rafe chuckled. "Sounds serious."

Avery took a sip of her drink and hummed in approval. "It was hard. Being the only child I wanted my parent's attention."

"Your father was busy politicking. What about your mother?"

"My mother passed away when I was fifteen."

"I'm sorry." He paused. "Mine did, as well."

"Sorry. At least you had your siblings."

"That I did." He chuckled. "There was always something going on at the Lawson house. Especially with my twin sisters, Desiree and Dominique."

"I always wished I had siblings."

"Be careful what you wish for," he teased. "Justin is the youngest so most of the time growing up, he wasn't involved in the craziness. Lee Ann is the oldest girl. She's married to a congressman and they're expecting twins."

"Wow!"

"Yeah, that's what we all said. Desi and Dom are married. Never thought we'd see Dominique settle down." He chuckled. "And Justin is working in law, much to the delight of my father."

"Holidays must have been great."

"Hmm, they usually start out that way."

"And then…"

"I might have one drink too many and say what I really feel," he said offhandedly, looked away then returned his attention to Avery.

"Does that happen often?" she hedged.

He shrugged slightly. "Only where my father is concerned. I make it a point to keep my distance and I think he prefers it that way."

"Why do you feel like that? You're his oldest son,

the heir, for lack of a better word. I would think there would be a natural bond."

Rafe tossed back the rest of his drink and set the tumbler down on the table. "Darlin', tonight is for new beginnings." He reached across the table and stroked her knuckles with the tip of his finger. "You good with that?"

Avery swallowed even as her heart leaped and banged in her chest. "Sure," she finally managed and realized in that moment the charisma of Rafe Lawson. He could be steadfast and charming all at once, making it, if not easy, necessary for you to agree with him.

"So...you were telling me earlier how you wound up in the Secret Service." He took up an oyster.

"Hmm, it was a combination of things, I suppose. I came from a household that was fueled by rules and discipline and regulations. I'm sure my father's line of work had a lot to do with that. Funny, you would think that a man who spouts democracy would run his home the same way."

"That wasn't the case."

"Not at all. My father...expected excellence in every aspect of my life. I was forever trying to prove myself to him—to rise to the occasion. All of that rigidity and discipline shaped me, I suppose."

"I would think you would have had enough of that, so how—no, why did you decide on the Secret Service? It's not a typical profession."

"For a woman?" she challenged.

"For anyone."

Avery brought the glass to her lips, hesitated, then took a sip. She slowly lowered the glass and set it down. "I can't say it was only the way I was raised." She glanced away for a moment. "I remember I was in high school and the nuns showed us a documentary on Kennedy."

"Nuns?" Rafe smirked.

"That's a whole other conversation. Anyway, I was fascinated by the response and the reaction of the Secret Service after the shooting. Instead of turning away from it, I wanted to be in a profession that required focus and discipline—things that I was used to. But I knew I didn't want to be a police officer. Much later, I was introduced to former Director Paulsen at a dinner. She was the first woman to hold the position. I was so impressed with her and her accomplishments that I knew I wanted to follow in her footsteps. She became my mentor and convinced me that, with my background and the fact that I am multi-lingual and have been entrenched in the surreal world of Washington politics, the Secret Service would be a perfect fit."

"Was your father satisfied?"

Avery lowered her gaze. "I'm sure he will be once I become director." She sputtered a laugh. "That will last for a while and then he will expect more."

"Sounds like you got yourself on a merry-go-round, darlin'." He drew circles on the table with his finger. "Round and round with no finish line. One thing I figured out a long time ago is the only person you can truly satisfy is yourself. If you spend all that energy trying to please someone else, fulfill their dreams..." He shook his head. "You'll make yourself crazy."

She expelled a breath. "Maybe."

Rafe studied the tightness that formed at the corner of her eyes and the way she pushed her food around on the plate. He'd stepped into one of those personal minefields and he had no intention of blowing this night up before it got started. "I speak two."

She glanced up from her plate. "Two?"

"Languages. English and Louisiana patois."

Avery laughed. "Good one." She pointed her fork at him. "I have to admit that patois is a beast to master. I've listened to friends from Louisiana or the Caribbean talk and when they get going I can't understand a damn thing they say."

Rafe tossed his head back and laughed. "You've got to get used to the rhythm is all. It's like music—different tempos, notes, highs and lows."

"Right." She shook her head. "That's the musician talking for sure."

He leaned forward. His eyes moved slowly over her face. "Life is all about rhythm, finding the beat that suits you and goin' with it. Once you figure it out the world looks a whole lot better."

"You make it sound simple."

"It can be, if you let it."

The deep ripple of his voice moved through her like the notes he spoke of, slow and measured, easing into unseen places. Her stomach fluttered and a wave of warmth flowed through her. The urge to touch him suddenly overwhelmed her. She reached for one of the oysters but he beat her to it. He lifted it between his fingers and brought it to her mouth. She sucked the delicacy from the shell and a slow, sexy smile formed on Rafe's face.

Avery knew this was the beginning of a memorable night for her.

Chapter 8

Throughout dinner they laughed and talked about everything from childhood memories to the state of the economy and the current president. They discovered that they both loved old movies and had traveled to many of the same places. Avery shared war stories of traveling with dignitaries, and Rafe added his own surreal memories of what it was like to sit across the dinner table from people he'd seen on television or who were written about in newspapers.

By the time they finished their three-hour dinner, Avery felt as if she'd been waiting for most of her life for him and the very idea frightened her.

"Someplace for a nightcap?" Rafe asked as they walked to his car.

Avery glanced up at him. "I'd like that."

Rafe took her hand. "Let's walk. Nice night."

Avery wrapped her fingers around his hand and allowed the electric warmth of his touch to sizzle right up to her lashes that fluttered for the briefest moment. Her heart leaped as she fell easily in step with him.

"Any place you prefer? It's been a while for me. In DC," he added with a half smile, "but I remember a place called The Hub."

Avery laughed. "You're kidding. My friend Kerry and I go there all the time."

"We might have been…what's that sayin', two ships passin' in the night?"

"Maybe."

"If I recall right it should be about two blocks down on M Street."

"Good memory."

"I remember the things that are important. If I had seen you…I would've never forgotten."

Avery's face heated. "I don't think I would have either," she said on a breath, surprising herself.

Rafe lightly squeezed her hand.

The Hub was a stark departure from Le Galleria. From the moment Rafe pulled open the smoked glass and chrome door they were greeted by the buzz of energetic conversation and the ebb and flow of raucous laughter, mixed with the soulful vibe from the live band. The artifice of practiced sophistication that was the hallmark of Le Galleria was nowhere to be seen among the pulsing crowd that stood or gathered at tables, leaned against walls and lounged at the bar.

A harried hostess snatched two menus from the holder. "Welcome to The Hub. It'll be about twenty minutes to a half hour for a table."

Rafe gave Avery a questioning look. "The bar is
fine." Avery nodded in agreement. He slid his arm
around her waist and guided her across the crowded
room to the bar. He stood behind her with his hands
on either side of her waist as she slid onto the bar stool.
She could feel the warmth of his breath against the back
of her neck. The air tumbled in her lungs.

"Your scent," he whispered right behind her ear then
dropped a featherlight kiss there, "is doing things to
me." He sat down and angled his body toward her.
The right corner of his mouth lifted ever so slightly.
"What're you having, darlin'?" He reached out and
stroked the curve of her jaw. He loved the way it felt
beneath his fingertip, hard and soft and smooth. He
watched her lips part and the pulse beat at the base of
her throat. He leaned forward, pulled by the invitation of her mouth. He barely brushed his lips against
hers, enough to be teased by the hint of sweetness
from her apple martini. The rules of chivalry that had
been drilled into him since he was old enough to talk
held him in check. Yet as much as he may desire to
take Avery to his bed, *this* was the part that he craved
most—the dance—the warm-up and rehearsal for the
main event. It was all about stoking desire so that there
was no other alternative than to accept what was inevitable. Sex was only the outcome, the release. But the
way to make it memorable and worth every hot breath,
every stroke was to work for the moment.

"What can I get you?" the waiter asked while he
wiped down the space in front of them with a damp
cloth. Like an illusionist a bowl of pretzels appeared
in his other hand.

"Apple martini for the lady. Bourbon on the rocks for me."

"When was the last time you were here?" Avery asked once the bartender moved away.

"Aw, wow, maybe a year or two. I don't get down here much unless I'm playing. My sister Lee Ann and her husband reside here, of course, but we all generally get together either because of family crisis or a holiday."

Avery leaned in to better hear him. Rather than the multitude of bodies and sounds being a distraction, it forced a kind of intimacy, compelled you to be close, and minimize the space in between. She placed her small purse on the bar top and Rafe began to play a slow, sensuous melody across her hand with the tip of his thumb. "I always wondered how the secret agents unwound. What else do you do?" He watched her eyes widen for a moment and caught the slight flutter of a nerve in her right cheek.

"Target practice on the gun range," she said, looking straight at him.

"Hmmm." A wicked smile tilted his full mouth and drew lines at the corners of his eyes. "Always hit your target?"

She slowly crossed her legs. "Always."

"Here ya go." The bartender placed their drinks in front of them. "Want anything from the kitchen? I can get you a menu."

"Nothing for me," Avery said.

"We're good, thanks." He lifted his glass. "To… more of the same."

Avery tilted her head in question.

"Been perfect so far."

She smiled and touched her glass to his.

"I played here once…hmm, maybe four years ago," he said, taking a look around.

"Really?"

He nodded. "I was working on some new music and tried it out here."

"And how did it go?"

"Great crowd. They seemed to like it."

"Did you always know that music was what you wanted to do?"

He glanced down for a moment then at Avery. "Yeah, I think so." His smooth dark brown brow tightened in thought. "I can't really say when…or how. I just knew." He smiled as a memory formed. "My mama had this piano. Ancient as all hell. I think she got it from her granddaddy, but she could play that thing like it was a brand-new baby grand. Used to listen to her. Learned to play by ear until I learned to read music. I still learn by ear." He chuckled. "One Christmas, I was about ten and the family had its usual fest… There were all kinds of celebrities, politicians roaming through the house." He sipped his drink. "Grover Washington, Jr. was one of the entertainers for the evening." He slowly shook his head and smiled. "When I heard him play 'Mr. Magic,' damn, I was hooked. Told my mama I wanted a sax and I wanted to play just like him."

"And of course you charmed your mother into getting you a saxophone." Her knee brushed against his.

"Something like that. My daddy didn't take it too well. Never was interested in my playing. All he wanted was to remind me day after day that I was next in line; that he'd built a legacy and it was my responsibility as his son to fulfill it. I swear I used to think that he dragged me from one stuff-shirt event to the next hoping that it would wash music out of my head."

"Clearly it didn't." She lifted her chin. "Made you more determined."

"Guilty as charged." He finished his drink.

"So…are you working on new material?"

"Supposed to be." He glanced off for a moment. "It's not coming together as I'd hoped. Been a few set-backs with studio time and really finding the piece that speaks to the whole album."

"What do you want it to say?"

"Possibility. I want every composition to speak to possibility."

"How much is completed?"

"About six pieces. I want to round it out to ten."

"Artists fascinate me with their ability to take what they think and feel and turn it into something tangible. Like magic."

"If only." He chuckled. "What about you? I see you have a piano at your place. Do you play or is it for show? What hidden magic do you have?"

"Hmmm, I wish I could say I did have exquisite talent. I play a bit but I'm rather ordinary, actually."

Rafe leaned in. "There's nothing ordinary about you." His gaze moved slowly over her face. "Don't let trying to meet daddy's expectations make you ever feel less than outstanding."

A lump formed in her throat. No one had ever said that to her, least of all her father. She'd spent her life always striving, having to be better than the best simply to get her father to give a nod of acknowledgment.

Rafe moved closer until all she could see was the dark veil of his lashes that shielded his eyes. The room disappeared. The noise became a distant hum as his mouth touched hers with purpose this time. There was no one in the world, in that crowded space, except the two of them.

When he threaded his fingers through the back of her hair, pulled her closer to seal their lips she may have whimpered, she wasn't certain.

Rafe eased away, heated her face with the shadow of a smile. He brushed his thumb across her bottom lip. "Ready?"

The question was a loaded one. Avery swallowed, and uncertain of her voice she simply nodded, yes.

Rafe took her hand and helped her to her feet.

They strolled back toward Le Galleria to retrieve his car as the essence of possibility sparkled between them with every step and every casual touch. Rafe knew this part of the dance. He'd tangoed more times than he'd ever admit for a variety of reasons; pure lust, because it was expected of him, and at times because he thought, although rarely, that he might want something more.

He glanced at Avery's profile. He was genuinely attracted to her. Reflexively his jaw tightened. Attraction. That was all. So what if he had Justin find out who she was, and so what if he flew across the country to have dinner with her. It was all part of the dance. Nothing more.

They stopped in front of the restaurant and Rafe handed over his parking stub to the valet.

"Thank you for tonight. It's been a while since I've had to get dressed up for dinner," Avery said with a smile.

"The Hub is really more my style. Guess I wanted

to impress you." Once he said the words, though off the cuff, he realized with a jolt that it was true. For reasons that escaped him, he did want to impress her.

Avery smiled up at him and he wanted to kiss her again, but didn't.

"I don't need to be impressed," she said softly.

When the questions in her eyes moved slowly over his face, Rafe retreated from her probing, her peeking behind his façade. He shifted his stance and winked. "I'll keep that in mind, darlin'."

The valet pulled up in front of them, hopped out and Rafe helped Avery into the car after a sizeable tip.

Rafe eased out into traffic and listened to "Heather," his British GPS, direct him to Avery's house. Generally, he let his inner compass guide him. He was pretty good with directions and remembering turns and shortcuts. But right now he didn't want to think about anything, least of all driving routes. He stole a look at Avery and immediately that feeling was back in his gut again. *Anticipation.* That was all it could be. He reached over with his right hand and covered hers that were nestled in her lap. Her head angled toward his and when she smiled it took pure willpower not to pull over.

"Music?" he asked.

"Sure."

She leaned her head back against the leather headrest and closed her eyes. Rafe drew in a long breath and refocused his attention to the road. Tonight they would have incredible sex, the itch that they both had would be scratched, he'd go back to NOLA and she'd go back to Secret Servicing and if by chance they ran into each other again they would talk, laugh, remember these moments, and maybe have lunch or a drink for old times' sake and then return to their lives. Because that was the only way it could be for him.

"You're looking very serious over there," Avery said, cutting into his thoughts. "Everything okay?"

He realized that he was actually frowning in concentration. "Everything's fine, just running some numbers through my head."

"About your album?"

"Hmm," he lied.

"You'll work it out. Sometimes all it takes is a change in atmosphere to get a different perspective. And you'll be back on track."

"You sound pretty sure."

"I am. I heard you play. I watched you perform, I listened to the passion in your voice when you spoke about music. I know all too well that feeling of wanting to get it 'just right.' Been there. Let it come. It will."

"I thought I was the one giving out the advice," he teased.

"Got to be able to take as well as give."

He paused a beat as a myriad of thoughts and images of her writhing beneath him ran through his head. "Yes, ma'am." The tip of his finger brushed across her knee and he would have sworn he heard her quick intake of breath or maybe it was his. The thought of just touching her skin set him off.

He made the turn onto her street. Avery shifted in her seat. Rafe pulled into the driveway of her town house. The locks disengaged. He turned off the engine, palmed the keys and got out. He came around to Avery's door and helped her exit. A look that bordered on anticipation and uncertainty flickered for an instant when the light from the streetlight caught her eyes. It would be up to her. It had to be. If this was what she wanted, she would have to let him know.

"Coming in...for a while?"

Rafe gave a slight, nonchalant shrug. "Getting late. You sure?"

She swallowed. "Yes. If you are." She held his gaze.

He nodded. "Whatever the lady wants."

He followed her up the short walkway to the front door.

Chapter 9

It had been a while since she'd brought a man home with the intention of going to bed with him. She was no prude by any stretch of the imagination, but when she did make this leap—she'd generally invested more time. She'd evaluate all the rights and wrongs, and weigh the pros and cons; yet even so in the back of her mind there always hung the question: Would her father approve? *Crazy.* She knew it was insane. She was a grown-ass woman. Yet the yearning for his approval forever nipped at her heels, whispered in her ear, nudged and pushed her. Except this time.

"Make yourself comfortable. I'm going to put my things down. Want a snack or anything, something to drink?"

"I think I can find my way around, if it's cool with you."

"Sure." She tugged in a breath and headed to her bedroom.

Avery quietly shut the door behind her. Her heart banged. Her eyes swept the room looking for anything out of place. She crossed the room while taking off her caftan and hung it in the closet, her shoes followed. These mindless activities didn't distract her from what was on the other side of the door.

She'd never considered herself a tease, but is this what she really wanted to do? Maybe she should go out there, have a quick nightcap and tell him what a great time she had and hope they can do it again sometime. After all, she barely knew him. Rafe had proven himself to be the consummate gentleman. He would understand. She gripped the edge of the dresser and faced herself in the mirror. Despite the lack of real time between them, she felt as if she'd known him forever. She'd wanted him from the moment she'd set eyes on him at his grandfather's party.

They were consenting adults. No one was talking about forever, just tonight. She pushed down the last vestiges of doubt, opened the door and walked out.

When she returned to the living room she stopped short in surprise.

"Hope you don't mind."

Rafe had prepared a platter of cheeses, fruit and crackers, located her long-stemmed wineglasses—that Kerry bought her for her last birthday—and set them out on the coffee table along with a bottle of wine. The music was on, low enough not to be a distraction, but just enough to provide a soothing backdrop. If she didn't know better she would have sworn that he'd also dimmed the lights, but her lights didn't dim.

He'd done all this as if he'd been to her home dozens of times, knew her likes and dislikes and could move among her things with a sense of ownership, yet at the same time seem totally unobtrusive. It was that *thing* about him, that self-assurance, the way he did what he wanted in such a way that you believed it was what you desired all along. And even if it wasn't what you envisioned it to be.

Avery walked fully into the room. Rafe picked up a glass of wine and handed it to her.

"Thank you for tonight." He tapped his glass to hers. "It was worth my staying in town." He took a sip from his glass.

She moved toward the couch and sat down. "Nice spread," she teased.

"Glad you like it." He lifted a cracker, added a piece of brie and brought it to her lips.

Slowly she opened her mouth and let the tiny delicacy slip across her tongue. "Hmm," she hummed.

He popped a grape into his mouth then spread a slice of cheddar onto a cracker and took a bite. He leaned back against the cushions of the couch. "You have a nice place, very you."

"Meaning?"

He draped his arm along the back and let his fingertips lightly tease the back of her neck. "Simple, straightforward and elegant. The piano speaks to the unawakened artist in you, while your furnishings reflect order and simplicity with the smooth lines, and the colors, soft and muted—" he angled his head, "—give the illusion of something just beneath the surface that can't quite be grasped."

His touch, his voice scrambled her thoughts. She

heard him and didn't hear him. It was as if he were waving a metronome in front of her to drag her deep under his spell.

She blinked rapidly to clear her head and reached for her glass of wine, nearly finishing it in one swallow. "I don't know if I ever thought about it that way."

"You just know what you like, what you want." It was more of a statement than a question.

Avery swallowed. "I'd like to think so."

Rafe brushed the pad of his thumb across her bottom lip. "And what is it that you want, Avery, right now, tonight?"

She looked into his eyes, felt the warmth of his closeness, inhaled the hypnotic scent that swirled around him, shut off her mind and listened to her body instead.

"I'd like you to stay with me tonight."

A slow smile curved his mouth ever so slightly. "Is it what you'd *like* or is it what you *want*?" His fingers continued their symphony on the back of her neck.

Her lids fluttered. "It's what I want," she said on a breath.

His jaw flexed and a raw rumble vibrated in his throat. He took her glass from her hand and placed it on the table. "Show me where you'd like me to stay."

She stood and extended her hand toward him. He took it and followed her to her bedroom.

Avery walked into her room. Her heart was beating so rapidly she could barely breathe. She heard the door shut behind them. She turned to face him. There was something dark and determined in his eyes, the set of his face. Her stomach fluttered.

Rafe's eyes rolled over her, heating every place that they landed. Her chest heaved with every breath.

"So glad you didn't go all cliché on me and change into something more comfortable." He moved closer. "I *want* the pleasure of undressing you."

He turned her around so that her back faced him. By degrees he unzipped her dress. As her bare skin appeared he placed hot, tiny kisses along her spine. The inside of her thighs quivered.

"Sweet," he murmured after each kiss. The dress fell to her feet. His hands moved languidly across her shoulders and down her arms. They stroked her waist and glided across her hips. He unsnapped her bra, kissed the back of her neck and inched the straps down while he pressed against her round derriere. She gasped, but he held her tightly around the waist with his arm. With his free hand he cupped the weight of her left breast and ran his finger across the nipple until it peaked.

Avery moaned and gripped his hand, holding it firmly against her while he kneaded it. Her body melded with his as she pushed back against him.

Rafe's hand drifted down across her belly and played with the elastic band of her panties before slipping beneath the frills. His talented fingers played with her, taunted her, became wet with her.

"Tell me what you want, darlin'," he breathed into her ear. "Whisper it to me."

His finger slid up inside of her. "Ahhh...you," she managed on a strangled breath. Her neck arched.

"Are you sure?"

"Yesss," she hissed from between her teeth. She was going to come all over him.

Two fingers now. The room spun.

Somehow Rafe was in front of her, his fingers back

inside her. In and out. His lips covered hers, his tongue taunted and danced in her mouth. Faster. A bit deeper. *Oh...god.*

She gripped his hand. Pressed it hard against her.

"Not yet, darlin'." He slowly removed his fingers. Avery cried out. "Shhh. Hush now." He slipped his wet fingers between his lips. "Hmm, just the way I imagined." Avery's entire body trembled. He hooked his thumbs over the elastic and tugged the lace and frill over her hips and down her thighs, moving down her body until he was on his knees in front of her.

Rafe firmly cupped the globes of her behind and pulled her toward his mouth. His tongue flicked across her throbbing clitoris and nearly sent her to her knees. He hummed against her with every lick, every suckle.

Her thighs trembled, her knees weakened. She felt her orgasm begin to rise again. This time from the soles of her feet. She wouldn't let him stop her from coming this time. She was sure she would lose her natural mind if he did.

The telltale quickening began. The teasing intensified. Avery's moans grew. She rocked her hips against him. *It wouldn't be long now.* Her head swam.

Everything stopped. Her eyes flew open. Rafe stood in front of her slowly unbuttoning his shirt. He took it off and casually walked across the room to place it on the chair by the window. Then came his belt. His pants followed, then his briefs.

When she'd imagined him wet and naked from the shower it could not compare to the real specimen in front of her. He was sculpted as if artists had spent their career in carving perfection. She didn't believe that he could possibly understand how beautiful he was. His hard, throbbing cock was beyond magnificent, menacing and thrilling to see.

She wanted him. She wanted him inside her. Deep inside. She needed to have the experience of what perfection felt like.

Rafe smiled almost shyly as he walked toward her. A smile that made her heart ache. For in that instant was a moment of vulnerability that she hadn't before seen in him and it made her want to fix whatever was broken, give him whatever it was that he needed.

He stepped up to her, cupped her cheeks in his hands and kissed her slow and deep. She tasted herself and him as he backed her up to her bed.

"Are you sure?" he asked again and took her hand to envelop his erection while he eased her onto the bed.

She stretched out atop the comforter and stroked him. "Very."

His jaw clenched and he sucked in air through his teeth as he positioned himself above her. He pushed her thighs apart with his knee, kissed the inside of her thighs while he lifted her legs over the bend in his arms, brushed across her sex with his lips, suckled her one last time.

Avery cried out as her insides clenched, needing the emptiness filled. She couldn't remember ever wanting someone so desperately that it left her unable to think of anything beyond getting satisfied.

And then she felt him. Her breath caught and held in her chest as he pressed against her wet opening. He lifted her legs higher until she was incapable of moving, totally open and ready. Still he waited.

He gave her just an inch more to open her. Her body

trembled. He kissed her deeply and then he filled her in a long hard thrust.

Rafe's ragged groan mixed with her muffled cry. Avery's eyes flew open. He looked down at her, into her. For a moment he didn't move. He held them suspended between exquisite bliss and release.

Avery channeled all her senses to her core and flexed her vaginal walls around his erection…once…twice.

Rafe's response was immediate and body shattering. The thrust, hard and deep, pushed the air from her lungs.

She held him as close to her as air would allow. The rush of sensations that flew through her with every move he made was beyond anything she'd experienced before it. It was exhilarating and frightening all at once, making her want to scream, cry, to tell him to wait, to tell him to never stop. Even as he moved inside her he made love to her whole body. He kissed her and nibbled her neck, teased her earlobes, laved her tender breasts with his tongue, caressed her body with strong expert hands that held her and moved her to his will. Between his own moans of pleasure he murmured how good she felt to him, how beautiful she was, that this time was for her, and to let go and let him have her.

Rafe bent his head and pressed his mouth to her ear, slid his hands beneath her hips and held her so that she could not move, but only feel him. "Surrender to me," he whispered deep in her ear.

The heat of his breath, the incredible way he flexed his shaft inside of her, the rush of sizzling sensations that raced through her from the bottom of her feet, pushed tears from her eyes. She was on a precipice, held there, terrified to leap and end this fantasy yet desperate to be released.

"Look at me," he whispered. He undulated his hips and stroked her in short bursts.

Avery could barely breathe. Her heart raced out of control. Her eyes fluttered open. There was that half smile that made her crazy.

"Now," he whispered and hit that spot inside of her that she'd only read about.

Her cry stuck in her throat as wave after wave of ecstasy rolled through her. Her body shook as if electrified while her insides sucked on him in a frenzy of release.

Rafe covered her mouth in a tender kiss as he continued to ride her through her climax, deeper and faster, his own breathing escalating.

Avery felt the change in him, the way his entire body hardened and his already thick cock stiffened even further inside her. His groan rose from deep in his belly. His fingers dug into her behind when his head reared back and release whipped through him like a Louisiana hurricane.

She held him, as the power of his coming flowed up and down his body, stole another release from her until he was spent.

Avery trembled even as she stroked his back, kissed him tenderly on his cheek, listened to his racing heart. Her own body remained in the throes of what they'd shared. She couldn't think or put words to how she felt, how he'd made her feel. It was surreal. She wanted to laugh and cry and sing and go into a corner and relive it all.

They lay for a while in the warmth of afterglow,

locked together until the spinning ceased and their heartbeats returned to normal.

Rafe kissed her cheek. "I'm gonna get up, cher," he said in a gravelly voice.

"Hmm," was all she could manage when he finally lowered her legs.

Rafe gingerly eased out of her, mindful of the very full condom, and stood up.

Avery watched him through half-opened eyes. He was beyond magnificent, that's all she had to say. She closed her eyes and turned onto her side.

Rafe stood under the beat of the shower as the room filled with steam. He always felt a sense of completeness after good sex, that empty spot in his soul momentarily filled. But this wasn't just good sex. It was something else and for the first time in longer than he cared to remember it seemed to mean more than just "getting off." It unnerved him.

He turned off the shower and stepped out. He took a towel, rubbed the fogged mirror and gazed at his hazy reflection. On the surface he looked exactly the same, but he wasn't. That was a problem. He dried off and returned to Avery's bed.

Chapter 10

Avery blinked slowly against the light that peeked through the blinds. She sighed. The nightstand clock read 7:00 a.m. She stretched. Her muscles ached deliciously. Her vagina throbbed. The night rushed back to her and she turned to find the space next to her empty, and for an instant she thought she'd only dreamed of her night with Rafe. But it wasn't a dream. She inhaled his scent on the pillow, on her body.

She sat up, tossed the sheets aside and got out of bed. His clothes were gone. Her heart pounded. She grabbed her robe from the hook on the back of her bedroom door and walked down the short hallway to the front of the house.

All remnants from their night before were gone: the wine, the glasses, the plate of snacks. She turned the corner and there he was in her kitchen.

He closed the refrigerator door and turned to her. "Mornin', darlin'."

The moment of panic she felt slowly subsided. "Hi."

"Hope you like omelets. I'm starved."

That smile again.

"I could eat," she said.

"Have a seat. Should be ready soon."

She bit back a smile as she watched him move around her space as if he'd always been there, belonged there. Every now and again, while he whipped the eggs and added the fixings he would look over and wink at her and her heart would sing.

"I'm heading back today," he said when he set her plate in front of her.

Her pulse jumped. "Of course. I'm sure you have tons of things to do."

"Yeah." He chewed slowly. "What are your plans for today?"

"Hmmm, not sure really. Probably get together with Kerry later."

He nodded.

"Maybe we can all do something…the next time you come down," she said, hedging.

"Maybe," he replied, uncommitted. He took his plate and put it in the sink.

"Thanks for cleaning up in the living room. You didn't have to do that. And breakfast. It was delicious."

He didn't respond.

Her heart started to race and she had the overwhelming feeling that she would burst out into tears any minute.

Rafe walked over to her, lifted her chin so that she

was forced to look into his eyes. He leaned down and kissed her lightly on the lips. "I'll call you."

Avery swallowed over the knot in her throat. "Sure. When you have time," she said as casually as she could manage.

His dark eyes roamed over her face for a moment and then he turned away.

She got up and followed him to the door.

"You be good now, cher. Don't hurt anybody with all that Secret Servicing."

She forced a smile. "I'll try."

He opened the door and stepped out into the warm sunshine, took the three steps to the ground, strode to his car and then he was gone.

Avery slowly closed the door behind her and the tears that she'd kept at bay rolled down her cheeks.

Rafe drove back to his Arlington home with the music blasting for the entire ride in the hope that it would drown out the noise in his head. When he finally arrived back to his retreat he stalked through the house like a man possessed. He couldn't rein in his thoughts or get his body to slow down. He should have made love to her again, he fumed while he tore out of his clothes and changed into jeans and a T-shirt. That way he could have gotten her fully out of his system and been done with it.

A fast ride on his motorcycle was what he needed. The rush of air, the exhilaration of racing around cars and trucks on the open highway always calmed him. He put on his boots and stormed off to the garage. His Harley gleamed in the light. He snatched up his helmet and got on, bracing the heavy machine between his thighs.

* * *

The wind whipped around him as he sped and darted between cars and trucks on the open highway. The rush of adrenaline fueled him, made him a risk to anyone in his way. The distraction of Avery flew out of his head as he bore down and focused on the road. The other vehicles on the road were mere flashes in his peripheral vision. He rode for more than an hour with no specific destination in mind or maybe it was the destination of temporary oblivion. That point in time and space where there were no thoughts, no worries, no decisions to be made.

By the time he pulled into his garage his body had calmed and his thoughts marched through his head in less disarray. But that stirring in his center persisted. He needed to distance himself from DC, get back home, back to reality.

After a quick shower and another change of clothes, he gathered his sax case and small carryall, locked up and drove to the private landing strip where his Cessna awaited. He confirmed his flight plan with the control chief and as the plane rose higher and the landscape of the nation's capital grew distant he realized that he was leaving behind more than a city.

Kerry put her tube-socked feet up on Avery's coffee table as she usually did and flopped back against the cushions of the couch. They'd just come back from a run.

"That was supposed to be a jog," Kerry groused. "Not a marathon."

Avery plopped down on the love seat and tucked her legs beneath her. She looked off into the distance.

"You're gonna tell me what happened last night. You've been stalling all day. Was it awful? 'Cause you sure as hell act like it. What did he do to you?"

Avery sighed heavily. "There was nothing awful about it," she said softly.

Kerry perked up. "So…spill."

"We… Dinner was great. We talked and laughed and talked. Went for a nightcap at The Hub. Come to find out it's one of his favorite spots, too."

"Get out," Kerry said with a laugh.

"Yep." She paused. "Anyway, we eventually came back here."

Kerry's eyes widened in delight. "Go on."

Avery slowly replayed the events of the evening, up to and including Rafe's departure.

"Girl, girl…" Kerry fanned herself. "I knew he would be something to reckon with. You can just see it in the way he walks," she said with an underlying growl in her voice.

"You need to stop," Avery sputtered over her laughter.

"So if he was so awesome and your vajaja is still humming his tune, why the sad face?"

Avery drew in a long breath and exhaled. "I don't know how to explain it," she began, trying to find the words. "Just a feeling that I have."

"Which is what—that he's the best thing you've had since the flood—and he's fiiine, and rich?"

Avery shook her head. "No, it's more than that."

Kerry leaned forward, studied the face of her friend. "What is it, A? Is there something you're not telling me?"

Avery blinked rapidly. "I just think it was a one-night stand for him. It was the way he looked at me, the way he acted when he left." She sniffed.

"Oh, girl, you knew that was a possibility," she said as gently as she could. "You are two grown folks that filled a need in each other. You were attracted to him and he was attracted to you. There's nothing wrong with that."

Avery pushed up from her seat and began to pace. "Don't you think I know that? I read about him—all that stuff you gave me, and I slept with him anyway."

"Did you ask yourself why?"

Avery pursed her lips for a moment. "When…I was with him…he didn't seem to be the way he was portrayed. He was kind and gentle, funny, sexy. He made me feel like I was the only person in the room. I thought…"

"You thought you would be different."

Avery rolled her eyes.

"Look, I know I was the one that told you to go for it. I guess I didn't think that you would take it for more than what it was—a night with an incredibly sexy man that you had the hots for and nothing more." She paused. "I'm sorry, sis."

Avery waved off the apology. "You don't have anything to be sorry for. Like you said, I'm a big girl." She heaved a sigh. "And I definitely needed a full tune-up." She grinned.

"Now that's what I'm talkin' about!" Kerry hopped up and went to hug her friend. "I think that deserves a toast."

They walked into the kitchen and Kerry took out two bottles of Perrier from the fridge.

"What are we toasting to?" Avery asked and sat down on the bar stool at the counter.

Kerry set two bottles on the counter, opened hers and took a long, welcome swallow. "To great sex any day out of the week."

Avery giggled. "To great sex." But even as she smiled and sipped her sparkling water she couldn't shake Rafe's sensual words from her head, *"surrender to me,"* because she knew she had done just that.

Chapter 11

Once he landed in Louisiana and picked up his SUV from the lot, he decided to drive over to the family home instead of going to his place. For reasons that escaped him he didn't want to go home.

Rafe pulled into the long driveway and parked, but was surprised to see an unfamiliar car—a black Lexus. Maybe one of his sisters had gotten a new ride, as he knew that Justin was out of town on business. He used his key and let himself in.

"Hello!" he called out. He heard the click of heels coming down the stairs. He glanced up and his entire expression bloomed in delight. "Aunt Jackie? What in the world are you doing here?"

She came down the stairs and into his embrace. She tiptoed and kissed his cheek. "Well, look what the devil dragged in." She stepped back and held him at arm's length. "My handsome nephew." She stroked his chin. "How are you?"

"A better question is, how are you?" He looped his arm across her shoulders and they walked into the sitting room.

Jacqueline Lawson was Branford's only sister. For years they'd been estranged. And Jacqueline, who had the same fire in her veins as her nephew, never let her non-relationship with her elder brother stop her from doing whatever the hell she wanted to. She was a renowned photographer that traveled the world, but when a near-death illness nearly took her from the family, she'd returned home for treatment and the wounds between her and her brother had been mended—at least for the most part. However, it was more than her brother's bone marrow that saved her, it was finding Raymond Jordan.

"So, what's going on? What brings you back to the old homestead?" Rafe poured himself a much-needed bourbon. Offered one to his aunt but she declined with a wave of her hand.

"I'm actually here on assignment. I'm doing a photo documentary of the rebuilding of the Ninth Ward after Katrina."

"Hmm." His right brow rose. "Unfortunately, you won't have much to shoot. The rehab is dismal at best." He leaned against the mantel and took a swallow of his drink.

"I know. That's what I want to show. Where did the money go, and more important, the people?" She crossed her legs and leaned back.

"How long will you be in town?"

"Couple of weeks, maybe more."

"Raymond can spare you for that long?" he teased.

"As a matter of fact…no, but that's what makes going back home so much fun." She gave him a wicked wink.

He totally adored his aunt. She was feisty and irreverent and down to earth all at the same time.

"I know why I'm here—decided why spend money on a hotel when there was this big-ass house? But what are you doing here? I know you have your place just outside of town."

"Hmm, just getting back from DC, actually."

Her eyes widened. "You went to see your father?" she asked incredulously. She knew how deep the divide was between father and son.

"No. I went to see a woman."

"Oh, that sounds more like you."

"Aunt J, whether you believe it or not I don't just run around, I actually put in work," he said with a grin.

"Hmm, umm. Is she stunning as all the others?"

He buried his focus in his glass. "Very," he said quietly.

"What's that I hear in your voice?"

He glanced over at his aunt. "Nothing. She's a beautiful woman."

"Where'd you meet her?"

"Here, actually."

"Oh, really?"

"During Granddad's birthday party. She was part of the Secret Service detail for the vice president."

Jacqueline tossed her head back and laughed. "Secret Service! You sure know how to pick 'em, nephew. Well, she must be something special to have you traipse all the way to DC. Tell me all about her. What's her name?"

He refilled his glass. "Avery Richards."

Jacqueline was quiet for a moment. "The name rings a bell. I'm not sure why."

Rafe shrugged. "She's Horace Richards's daughter, if that means anything."

"Oh." She lowered her head.

"What?"

"Are you serious about her?"

"We've been out on one date."

"And I assume you slept with her."

"A gentleman never tells." He waited. "Is there something that I should know?"

"If you're not serious about her then it doesn't really matter."

"What if I was?"

"Are you?"

"Aunt J, just tell me what you're dying to tell me anyway. Cut to the chase."

Jacqueline linked her fingers together. "Your father and Horace Richards go way back—and not in a good way."

Rafe strolled over to the armchair and sat down. He crossed his right ankle over his left knee. "I'm listening."

She pushed out a breath. "Back in law school your father and Horace were best friends. They did everything together, including wanting to forge a political career. But they were competitive. I mean diehard competitors. They constantly one-upped each other."

"Interesting friendship."

"That's an understatement. Anyway, the competition spilled over into their private lives. Your father and Horace were at a party. Your mother was there with her friend Juliette. Louisa caught the eye of them both."

Rafe grinned, envisioning his mother as a young beautiful woman, and turning the head of his father.

"Anyway, Horace moved on Louisa first. They went on a few dates but it didn't work out. Apparently the reason was your father. They started seeing each other and the rest turned into the five of you."

"So, I don't see the problem. They got married."

"It was a problem for Horace. He started dating Juliette, maybe to stay close to Branford. But he built up this almost irrational disdain for your father. I remember overhearing them arguing one night shortly after your father proposed to your mother. Horace accused your father of betraying him, of sneaking behind his back with Louisa and making a fool of him in front of all of their friends even though your father knew how Horace felt about your mother. Your father wanted to know what his problem was since he was dating Juliette, only to have Horace say that was because she couldn't have Branford, as well."

"Whoa. Is it true?"

Jacqueline shrugged. "You know your father. He keeps his own counsel."

"All I know is that whenever I saw Branford with your mother he was happier than any other time. Louisa brought out a side of your father that he always kept hidden. Anyway, Horace came to the wedding with Juliette, and they eventually got married. But things were never the same between them." She paused. "I know you pretty much steer clear of your father and what he does on Capitol Hill, but your father is up for Chairman of the Homeland Security Committee."

"And?"

"So is Horace Richards."

"Oh." His brows arched. He stood. "Well, may the best man win, I guess." He finished the rest of his bourbon.

"Your father will spiral into one of his tirades when he finds out you're seeing Horace's daughter."

"Not that it would bother me, but I never said I would see her again."

"You will." She gave him a knowing look. "If you hadn't planned to before—I know you, nephew—you'll see her just to spite your father."

He chuckled. "You wound me, Auntie." He dramatically held his hand to his chest.

"Your auntie tells you the truth." She pushed up from her seat and walked up to him. She looked deep into his eyes. "Don't let the messiness with you and your dad spill on that woman." She lightly pinched his cheek. "I'm going to take a nap. I'm beat. Are you staying? Maybe we can order something for dinner later. I'm not up for cooking."

"Sure. Sounds good. Go rest. We'll talk later."

Jacqueline turned and walked out.

Rafe slid his hands into his pants pockets and walked to the window. He stared out onto the sprawling lawn and let his mind process everything his aunt told him.

Rafe spent the following day working in the studio with his producer. They'd been at it since early morning. Although they'd made some progress and were satisfied with the pieces that were laid down, the new work still seemed to be out of reach.

"Let's call it a day," he said to the engineering crew and the four-piece band. "Good work, everybody. Thanks."

"When do you want to come back?" his engineer asked.

"Give me a week or so. I think I'm gonna take a short trip and get my head together. I'll call you."

Everyone packed up and began to file out. Rafe was the last to leave. He'd driven his Harley and now wished that he hadn't. The weather had gone from balmy to stormy. The wind and rain made riding hazardous, but he didn't have much choice. The usual twenty-minute trip took twice the time and he was relieved when he finally pulled into his garage.

He got out of his wet clothes and went to fix something to eat. But the moment he was alone and without the distraction of composing and playing then riding, his thoughts sped back to Avery. He had yet to call her as he said he would. Generally he never told a woman something that he didn't mean or intend to do. He wasn't sure why he hadn't called Avery. It wasn't as if she didn't constantly occupy his thoughts. Maybe that was it. He was giving her more space in his head than he was ready to deal with.

He thought about what his aunt told him about his father and Avery's dad. Part of him wanted to pursue the relationship if for no other reason than to piss off his father. But he didn't want that to be the motivation. Not totally. It was, however, an incentive.

He took a steak out of the freezer and put it in the sink under running water. What he needed to do was get Avery out of his system. He turned off the water, dried his hands on a towel and pulled out his cell phone from his pocket.

He hadn't seen Miranda in several months. Only a few "checking-in" text messages. Hopefully she was available for a late dinner. Miranda was always great company, and she hated strings as much as he did.

That night it was Miranda. Days later it was Celeste, then Tess then Lindsay. He flew down to Acapulco for a weekend with friends in the hope of unwinding. When he finally slowed down he realized that he was still unsettled. Beautiful, sexy women, intelligent conversation, exotic locations, none of it meant anything. He wined and dined them and kissed them good-night, even though they were ready for more from him. As much as he believed that what he wanted was someone other than Avery Richards, he was wrong.

It had been nearly three weeks since he'd seen or spoken to her. She'd probably moved on.

He paced across his bedroom floor staring at his phone. He pushed out a breath of frustration, then tossed the phone onto the bed and headed to his home gym.

Chapter 12

"From the look on your face I take it you haven't heard from him," Kerry said.

"No, but I've seen him. In the weekly tabloids." She sputtered a fake laugh. "Each time with someone new." Avery pushed the salad around on her plate. "But, it's okay. Like you said, I'm a big girl."

"Mmm-hmm." She took a sip from her glass of water. "If it didn't matter you wouldn't have been walking around for the past month in a daze. And what if he were to call you…?"

Avery lifted her eyes from her plate. "What?"

Kerry raised her chin toward the door. Avery turned around and her heart stood still.

Rafe walked toward their table and stopped next to Avery. "Your office told me where I could probably find you."

"Maybe I need a new assistant," she said tongue in cheek.

"Good to see you again, Kerry."

"Rafe."

"Mind if I join you ladies?"

"Actually, I have to get back," Kerry said and ignored the death stare from Avery. She took some money from her purse and put it on the table. "I'll see you back at the office. Good to see you, Rafe. Look after our girl here." She pushed back from her seat and stood, squeezed Avery's shoulder and walked out.

Rafe rounded the table, pulled out the chair and sat down. "How are you?"

"Fine."

He slowly nodded. "I should have called you."

"No worries. I've seen that you've been busy. What are you doing here?"

Rafe rocked his jaw. "I came to see you."

"Why?" She wrapped her hands around her glass to keep them from shaking.

"Let's talk about it over dinner."

"No."

He paused, pursed his lips. "Okay. Understood."

That smile. Her heart banged.

Rafe pushed out a breath. "It was good to see you, Avery. I mean that."

The timbre of his voice dipped down into her soul and stirred up all the feelings and thoughts that she'd shoved away. She followed him with her eyes until she couldn't see him anymore.

She slammed her hand on the table, rattling everything.

* * *

Rafe strolled down Pennsylvania Avenue past the White House and the daily stream of tourists. The Capitol was in the distance. He checked the time.

He'd guessed that Avery wouldn't necessarily welcome him with open arms, but he'd underestimated her level of being pissed off. Seeing him with other women he was sure didn't help, not that he'd done anything to stop the photo hogs from snapping his picture. In the back of his mind he was fine with it. He wanted Avery to find out. It would ensure his one-way ticket to freedom. But once he had it in his hand he knew he should have never pursued it. He picked up his pace.

"Senator Lawson, your son is here to see you."

"My son?" he said into the intercom.

"Yes, sir."

He cleared his throat. "Send him in."

Rachel, his secretary, opened the door, stepped aside and let Rafe enter. She closed the door quietly behind her. Branford closed several manila folders on his desk before acknowledging him.

"Rafe. This is a surprise." He stood.

Rafe walked across the room and shook his father's hand. "You're looking well."

"What brings you back to DC?" He took a seat behind his desk.

Rafe took a seat. "Came to see a friend."

"A woman, no doubt," he said with a hint of sarcasm in his voice.

"You said 'back,'" he returned, ignoring the barb.

"I'd heard you were here a few weeks ago. Played at

some club in Georgetown. One of my staff happened to be in the audience."

Rafe chuckled. "Of course."

"So, you're back and you're here."

"I thought since I had a little more time I should at least see you."

"So who is she?" Branford asked, dismissing his son's pretense at congeniality.

Rafe almost smiled. "Avery Richards."

Branford's eyes flashed. "Avery Richards. Horace Richards's daughter?"

"From what she told me." He watched his father's expression tighten then relax.

"Secret Service. A little out of your comfort zone." He rocked back in his swivel chair and stroked his hairless chin.

"Didn't plan it that way."

Branford waved his hand. "How long will you be in town?"

He thought about Avery's reaction, the chill she gave off. It was going to take a while.

"Not sure. I'm going to stay in Arlington."

Branford nodded then stood, signaling that the impromptu meeting was at an end. "Maybe we can grab a drink or dinner at the club."

Rafe stood. His father almost sounded like he meant it. A part of him wanted him to mean it, but that was wistful thinking. "Sure. I'll call you."

Branford walked his son to the door. He clapped him heartily on the back. "Take care of yourself, son."

"Yeah, I will."

Branford closed the door and returned to his desk. He pressed the intercom.

"Yes, sir."

"Get me the background on an Agent. Avery Richards."

"Right away, sir."

Branford's jaw tightened as he looked off into the distance.

Rafe strolled down the long corridor, lined with the offices of those who held the world in the palms of their hands. The presence of wealth and power, mixed with arrogance and entitlement assaulted him. He snatched the visitor badge off his jacket, signed out on the log book and stabbed the button for the elevator.

He looked around at the thousand-dollar suits and designer white shirts, the secretaries that scurried back and forth or trailed their bosses. The Secret Service who stood as sentinels every few feet. His jaw tightened.

The elevator door opened. He stepped on and let the closing door seal him from all the trappings that had taken away the one thing he'd ever needed after his mother died. But the pull of this city, this place and all that it represented was stronger than any thread that bound Branford Lawson to his family.

Avery returned to her office. Kerry was in there waiting for her.

"Well?"

"Don't well me. Some friend. Why did you leave me like that?"

"Because you needed to talk or cuss him out or whatever, and I didn't need to be there. So…what happened?"

Avery rolled her eyes. "Nothing."

"What the hell does that mean?"

"He asked me to dinner…to talk."

"And?"

"I told him, no."

"W-what? Why?"

"He walked out of my house almost a month ago. I haven't heard a damned word from him. Yet he's running all over the place with one woman or the other." She shook her head vigorously. "No, I'm not going down that road with him. Rafe Lawson…he's not…"

"Not what? When did you all have a conversation that you were exclusive?"

Avery's lips tightened.

"Well?"

She huffed. "Whatever. Look, it could never work for all kinds of reasons."

Kerry stared at her for a moment. "Okay, girl." She got up. "I'm on duty in twenty minutes. I'm on overnight."

"I have to escort the VP to a congressional hearing at three. Then I'm done."

"We'll talk later or tomorrow."

"Sure."

Kerry walked out.

Avery shoved her purse into her desk drawer then kicked it shut. Why the hell did he have to show up? Just when the dreams of him were getting dim and the scent of him was finally out of her pores he turned up as if nothing had happened, as if he'd never said "I'll call you." But she'd known, she'd sensed that he wouldn't even while she'd hoped that she was wrong.

Her desk phone rang.

"Agent Richards. Yes. I'll be right there." She checked her service weapon in her shoulder holster and her backup, grabbed her suit jacket from the hook by the door and walked out.

"Avery."

She slowed and glanced over her shoulder. "Boss wants to see me, Mike."

He fell in step beside her. "Everything good?"

"Yes. Fine."

"I see you're covering the VP this afternoon."

"Committee meeting."

"Doing anything later…for dinner?"

"I… I have plans for this evening."

He bobbed his head. "Maybe some other time." He turned off and walked down the opposite corridpr.

Avery shook her head. She didn't know what to make of Mike these days. She thought she liked him better when he was an obnoxious pain in the ass. This Mike she couldn't put her finger on.

She tapped on the director's door.

"Come in. Close the door."

Avery came fully into the room.

"Please sit, Agent Richards."

Director Fischer was a decent enough guy. Not a people person, but he knew every angle of the job. He was a master at moving agents into just the right spot, giving them the assignments that were perfect for their temperament. He knew the law inside out and the personalities and proclivities of everyone the agents were assigned to cover.

"I asked you here to talk with you about your assignment."

"Yes, sir."

"How are things going with your new detail?"

"So far everything is fine. The VP has had a pretty light schedule."

"That's what I want to speak with you about."

"Yes?"

"You've been with the service for…" he turned to his computer screen, "six years."

"Yes, sir."

"Your reviews have been exemplary."

"Thank you, sir."

He leaned back and linked his fingers across his stomach. "You were former Director Paulsen's protégé. She thought very highly of you, said you had the potential to rise high up in the ranks."

Where was this going?

He cleared his throat. "Your father and I don't always see eye-to-eye, but he's a good man, very influential."

Avery shifted a bit in her seat.

"I mention your father because I don't want you to think that who he is will influence any decisions made."

"Decisions, sir?"

"As you know the agency is expanding as the need has presented itself. As a result there will be an Assistant Deputy Director position available in the coming months. You are being considered for that position along with two other candidates."

Avery's stomach fluttered. "Thank you…"

"There will be an extensive internal review and vetting. With all of the divisiveness in Washington and accusations of cronyism we want to make certain that we cross every 't' and do not leave any room for questions about who is in a leadership role here at the agency."

"I understand."

"Well." He flattened his palms on the desk. "That will be all, Agent Richards."

Avery stood. "Thank you, sir." She turned and walked out, breezed by Director Fischer's secretary and out into the main corridor. Her thoughts raced around in her head as she replayed the conversation. *Assistant Deputy Director.* Although there were others who held the title, they all reported directly to Fischer and they oversaw their own teams of agents. Yes, yes, yes! This is what she worked her ass off for. From Assistant to Deputy to Director. She could see it in her future.

She pressed for the elevator. The doors opened and Mike stepped off.

"We have to stop meeting like this." He stepped out and held the door for her. "He in a good mood?" Mike asked.

"Who?"

"Fischer. Just got a call to come up and see him."

"Oh." She stepped onto the elevator. "His usual self." She pressed the button for her floor.

Mike let the door close.

Avery stepped back and leaned against the far wall. Mike going to see Fischer could only mean that he was being considered, too. Damn!

Rafe returned to his home in Arlington and was relieved to see that the fridge and cabinets were stocked, fresh linens were put out and a handwritten note from Alice told him that she'd made his favorite, a pot of jambalaya, and it was in the fridge. She had to take her mother to the doctor but assured him that she was available if he needed her.

He smiled, folded the note and stuck it in the kitchen drawer. Alice was a pure gem.

He moved through the rooms and realized that even though it felt lived in, it was empty. A four-bedroom house with no one but him in it. The sad reality of it hit him unexpectedly. A wave of despondency swept through him.

What was he doing here? What was he doing with his life? He pretended that he didn't care, that living his life out loud was "his thing." He knew the truth. Everything he did was some form of rebellion, a middle finger, all designed to keep any real feelings at bay. The booze, the women, the risk-taking. All of it.

Then all of a sudden there she was and the safety nets that he'd wrapped around himself began to shred. So he did what he'd always done. He created distance to give himself a graceful out. And he was still doing it when he purposely went to see his father and dropped Avery's name.

He wasn't even certain what it was about Avery that had him twisted in a knot and questioning his motives, second-guessing his actions. It had been nearly sixteen years since he'd opened himself up to anyone and with good reason. He never wanted to feel that kind of pain again and the only way to ensure that was to not feel, at least not feel below the surface. He'd been successful. He'd lived his brand of happy. But looking around, hearing the echoing emptiness he realized that perhaps he really had not lived at all—only existed.

Avery was to blame for this rude awakening, and the only way to return to his comfort zone was to get Avery Richards out of his system once and for all.

Chapter 13

Avery slept in, thankful for a weekday off. She'd had a restless night, her thoughts swimming between Rafe's sudden appearance and her meeting with Fischer. Her temples still throbbed and she wasn't sure which bothered her most, seeing Rafe or the idea that she and Mike may very well be up for the same job.

Her meeting with Director Fischer replayed in her head and the smug look she received from Mike the prior afternoon didn't help to allay her concerns about her chances at the position. Neither of them mentioned the details of their meeting, but she was certain that he'd been advised as she was.

The hard truth was that it was difficult even under the best of circumstances for women within the agency. The Secret Service was holding on tooth and nail to the old boys' club. Director Paulsen made a crack in the ceiling but in terms of hierarchy within the agency it stopped and went with her when she stepped down—especially under the cloud of the security issues that happened under her watch. She assumed a tough position when she was appointed by the president, having to take over an agency that had major budgetary issues and personnel cuts, and was faced with unprecedented threat levels. It was almost as if she was set up to fail and in doing so, would seal the fate of any other woman who aspired to ascend the ladder.

But in the three years since she'd left, the agency had been retooled, the agents retrained and the departments reorganized. Now that the foundation was strong again the climb might not be as difficult.

The one bright light in this tunnel was that concentrating on her career would keep her mind off Rafe and the fact that she'd let him walk away. Every time she thought about it she could kick herself.

Avery opened the fridge and took out some eggs and English muffins. She prepared her eggs for a simple cheese omelet when the bell rang.

Perfect. She'd scheduled the cable company to come out and switch out her router. That would hopefully resolve the issue of why her reception was so spotty. They'd actually arrived at nine instead of five. Miracles still happened.

She wiped her hands on a towel and went to the front door.

"Your assistant said you were off today."

Her pulse galloped in her veins. She wanted to be pissed off and at the same time, she wanted to release the bubbles of joy that rose from her center.

She placed her hand on her hip. "I am definitely

going to have to report the help." She held on to her smile.

Rafe held up two cups of coffee. "I came bearing gifts."

When he looked at her like that with that glow in his eyes and the smile on that mouth, she knew she was pretty much helpless against it.

"Fortunately for you, I haven't had my morning coffee yet." She accepted one of the cups from his hand and stepped aside to let him in.

Rafe strolled into the living room. He set his cup down on the side table.

Avery drew in a steadying breath and shut the door and followed him inside.

Rafe turned toward her. "I'm sorry."

The words were so soft, so heartfelt that it sounded like a prayer. Avery's heart fluttered. She bit down on her bottom lip.

Rafe took a step toward her. "I should have called you. I shouldn't have let you think for a minute that what happened between us that night was anything but extraordinary." He reached out and touched her cheek. Her breath hitched. "Because it was, Avery. At least for me."

Her throat tightened. "Me, too."

There was that slow drag smile, rising easy like the sun and warming her from the inside out.

He held her face in his hands. "Let's start again."

She bobbed her head.

"Yeah?"

"Yes," she managed.

He brushed his thumb across her bottom lip and she shivered.

"I'm going to kiss you. Is that all right, cher?"

"Yes," she said on a breath.

But it wasn't a kiss. It was a conquering. It eased in on her, slipped around her, weakened her defenses and left her wanting to do whatever was needed to please her captor.

"I'm sorry," he whispered against her mouth.

She hungrily swallowed the words and they gave her soul sustenance. They guided her arms around his neck and melded her body into his. Damn, she gave in easy, but what the hell. She hummed her joy against his mouth.

Rafe eased away and looked into her eyes. He tenderly brushed a curled loop of hair away from her face. "How 'bout we really start again, darlin'." He subtly rocked his pelvis against her.

Avery grinned. "Okay."

Rafe straightened and dramatically cleared his throat. "I'm Raford Beaumont Lawson. My friends call me Rafe."

"Avery Michelle Richards," she said, biting back a grin.

"My pleasure, darlin'."

"Beaumont?" she teased with a sparkle in her eyes.

He chuckled lightly. "After my granddad, Clive."

"It fits you," she said, giving him the once-over.

"Is that right," he said and moved in on her.

She sucked in a breath.

"Now that we have formalities out of the way," he said and stroked her neck with his lips, "maybe we can work on getting to know each other better...this time."

Her body shivered. "What do you suggest?"

"Tell me your plans for today."

She craned her neck back and looked up at him. "Plans?"

"Yeah, what were you planning to do today on your day off?"

Was he punking her? "Weeeell, finish fixing breakfast, wait on the cable guy, ummm, clean out my fridge, go to the gym and…maybe watch a movie."

"Cool. Sounds like we have a full day." He headed toward the kitchen. "What do you want for breakfast?" he called out.

All she could do was laugh and go with the flow. He was settling down in her heart and making it very hard not to love him.

They worked together whipping up Rafe's breakfast specialty and this time he added cheese grits that had Avery salivating. He'd said it was his mother's recipe and one of his favorite comfort foods.

Even though they'd been out of each other's space for a month or more it was as if no time had separated them. The conversation was easy, the laughter so natural, the light touches and the smiles genuine.

"How is the music coming?" Avery asked while she loaded the dishwasher.

"Hmm, made a little progress. Still not where I want to be." He wiped down the table with a damp cloth.

"Progress is progress. Big or small."

He grinned. "Yeah it is, isn't it? Every little bit," he said, easing up behind her. He slid his arms around her waist. "I've been distracted."

Avery closed the dishwasher door and turned into his embrace. "Why? Distracted by what?"

"You, mostly." He pushed up against her, pinning her between his body and the dishwasher.

Her eyes widened. "Me?"

"Besides trying to find my creative mojo... I had *you* on my mind, darlin', and how I'd screwed things up."

She studied his expression then cupped his cheek in her palm. "Now that you're here, maybe you can start making it up to me...for screwing up," she said on a husky whisper.

His eyes darkened as the hint of a smile lifted the corner of his mouth. "How much time you have?"

"As long as it takes."

"My mama always said give a lady what she asks for. So, tell me, cher, what does the lady want?"

She leaned up. "You can start with this?" She brought her lips to his and it was all the encouragement that he needed.

Rafe hugged her to him, cutting off the air and space between them, more than happy to comply and will her body to succumb to his will, his every touch, kiss, murmur in her ear. He played with her mouth and teased her lips with his tongue.

Avery moaned. She felt his desire for her and still he held back, intent on the slow game of seduction.

His hand slid up under her T-shirt, caressed her heated skin, raised goose bumps of desire on every spot he touched. The tips of his fingers outlined the undersides of her breasts before sneaking around her back to unsnap her bra. Her breasts seemed to sigh in relief and rose to enjoy the thrill of his caress.

Rafe lifted her shirt, tugged it over her head and tossed it onto the counter. Her bra followed. He captured one peak between his lips and stroked it with the very tip of his tongue. Avery's body shook. He did it again and again before sharing the pleasure on the other side.

Avery's fingertips pressed into his shoulders.

He tugged on the string of her sweatpants and inched the elastic down across her hips, taking her panties with them. Down on his knees he tasted her, and a sudden powerful orgasm tore through her.

"Ahhhh...ahhhh." Her entire body trembled as he delved deeper and release swept through her in waves.

Weak in the aftermath, all she could do was hold on when he easily lifted her and draped her legs over his arms. He ripped open a condom and sheathed himself before he entered her.

Bright lights popped behind her lids with each powerful thrust that threatened to take her over the edge once again.

Avery kissed his cheeks, his mouth, held his head as he moaned, each stroke deeper and stronger. This was purely for him, she realized as his grip tightened and the pace quickened. She turned her body over to him completely, totally opening her spirit to let him in.

"A—very!" Again...again...again, until he was spent. His head dropped to her shoulder as the last of his essence pulsed out of him. "Damn, darlin'," he groaned. He lifted his head and looked into her eyes. He sucked her bottom lip, trailed kisses along her neck.

Her walls contracted. Rafe groaned. She offered him the fruit of her breasts and he hungrily feasted, setting off the rippling inside her that gripped and released him.

Tears of rapture sprang from the corners of her eyes

as he began to move inside her once again. All she could do was surrender to the pleasure that he gave her.

Avery lay curled on her side with Rafe spooned against her. He was insatiable. From the kitchen to the living room to her bedroom without the slightest indication that he was in any way satisfied.

Her body moaned, weak as a newborn. She felt his erection press against her. Rafe slid one leg between hers and cupped the weight of her breast in his palm.

"You make me crazy," he breathed into her neck. He tugged the sheet that was down around their hips and pulled it up to cover them. "Crazy," he whispered. He settled against her.

Avery couldn't keep her eyes open as Rafe's soothing heartbeat and steady breathing lulled her to sleep.

Chapter 14

After a much-needed nap followed by a thrilling shower together, Avery and Rafe padded off to the kitchen to whip up lunch. The cable repairman arrived in the meantime and changed Avery's router and reset her system.

They took their roasted chicken sandwiches and curled up on the couch to watch season three of *House of Cards*. Avery was both surprised and tickled that Rafe was a rabid fan even though he had so much disdain for what his father did and politics in general. Perhaps the fictionalized version of the backdoor double-dealing in the nation's capital validated his real-life misgivings.

"One of the elements that really gets to me are the winks and nods at Shakespeare," Rafe said. He took a bite of his sandwich and chewed thoughtfully, then pointed to the screen. "See right there? Spacey turns to the camera and talks directly to the audience. Totally Shakespeare."

Avery chuckled. "I thought I was the only one who noticed that! And what about the underlining concept? Husband and wife take over the government—totally *Macbeth*."

"Yes!" Rafe slapped his thigh and tossed his head back with laughter. "Exactly."

They shook their heads in amusement, then looked at each other and broke into laughter again.

"Great minds…" Rafe said. He draped an arm around Avery's shoulder and eased her close.

"Think alike," she said finishing the age-old adage. "I wouldn't take you for a fan of Shakespeare. More of a *Sons of Anarchy* kind of guy."

Rafe chuckled. "I have all kinds of hidden surprises, darlin'." He kissed her forehead. "Don't want to scare you off, but Jax Teller is my hero," he teased, referring to the leader of the rogue motorcycle gang.

"I can kinda see that," she said with a grin. "But it took me a minute to get used to Peg from *Married with Children* as Gemma Teller, the double-crossing, obsessive head of the family."

"Yeah, that Gemma is a piece of work. Never want to get on her wrong side."

They continued watching the episode, commenting and joking along the way.

Avery had never felt more comfortable with someone. Rafe was funny, smart as hell, considerate, sexy and an incredible lover, everything that a woman could want. The more they talked the more they discovered all that they had in common, from travel to books, world issues to television shows. The men she'd sporadically dated usually left much to be desired. Either they were closet chauvinists, were with her because of her father or simply did not turn her on in the least. Rafe Lawson was almost too good to be true. And even though his somewhat checkered reputation preceded him, he'd proven to be none of the things the tabloids said about him. Yet she couldn't shake the feeling that there was something beneath the surface. It was the faraway look in his eyes at times. As if he'd disappeared and gone to a place that didn't include her, even as he seemed to be attending to her every need. She wanted to simply "go with it" and relish the moment, but the pessimist in her, that part that was trained to spot possible danger, was waiting for the other shoe to fall.

"Do you want anything more to drink?" she asked when the episode ended.

"No. I'm good." He turned to her. "Actually, I need to get back home. I plan to fly out in the morning."

"Oh…sure."

"As a matter of fact, I should be getting over to my place." He pushed up and stood. "Have some things to take care of."

She glanced up, working to keep her expression neutral. "Yeah, I have things to do around here, as well."

He reached out. She placed her hand in his and he pulled her to her feet. "'Preciate the hospitality, darlin'," he said, in the raw lazy voice that thrilled her to her toes. *That grin*.

Avery tugged in a long breath. "It's been my pleasure."

"I aim to please." He leaned down and kissed her lips. "Anything you need me to do before I head out?" He held her at her waist.

"No. Go," she said, waving him off.

She walked with him to the door. He took his jacket from the coat rack and turned to her.

"I'll call you."

"Mmm-hmm."

"Promise." He kissed her again, opened the door and stepped out into the waning light.

She watched him as he walked to his car, got in and drove off. Right before she closed the door she noticed a dark sedan parked across the street. She thought she saw the image of a driver behind the tinted windows. Her antenna went up for a moment, but she shrugged it off and shut the door.

The drive back to Virginia gave him some time to clear his head and put some much-needed distance between him and Avery. He could easily find himself totally involved with her—if he allowed it. And he couldn't. He'd promised himself that he wouldn't go down that path again. Seeing her, being with her, was at first to stem his curiosity. Then it was to tick off his father after he'd found out about the rivalry that existed between his father and hers.

Well, his curiosity had been quelled and his father, surprisingly, didn't seem moved one way or the other. So what motivation did he have to pursue this thing between them?

An image of Avery's smile, her voice, the way she felt when he was inside her, the scent of her that still clung to him told him a different story, one that he was unwilling to confront. Yeah, he needed to get home, pack a bag and hit the road again.

Quinten was back in New York. Maybe he'd pay him

a visit, hit some clubs, take him up on his offer to use his studio and hopefully make some music. He'd also received an invitation from Melanie Harte to one of her legendary soirees. He smiled. Melanie's business The Platinum Society specialized in making connections between the elite clientele. Mel might even be able to hook him up with the perfect catch to get his mind and his body disconnected from Avery Richards.

Rafe spent maybe an hour puttering around the town house and making some calls to arrange to have the Cessna flight plan ready for departure back to Louisiana. He checked in with Quinten, who was more than happy to hang with his buddy, and as always, Melanie was planning a get-together and would be happy to have a sit-down with him. With his plans set, he grabbed his bag and sax case, left a thank-you note for Alice and headed out to the airport.

There was nothing quite as thrilling or as freeing as soaring above the earth, seeing the ground disappear beneath you, while the only thing keeping you in the air was skill, engineering and the Almighty.

He'd started taking flying lessons when he was sixteen after being introduced to a pilot during Career Day at his high school. He'd never forget Hugh McDonald. He must have been about seventy-five at the time he came to visit, but the teenage girls swooned over him as if he'd walked out of the movie screen and into their classroom. He remembered thinking "That old man ain't about nothing." He made up his mind to slouch in his seat and remain as disinterested as possible. But then Hugh began to talk about his experience as a Tuskegee Airman and what it was like for African American men in the military who had to not only fight the enemy abroad but the ones at home who believed that they didn't have the skills or the intelligence to fly a plane. He talked about his first mission with the 99th Fighter Squadron that was deployed in 1943.

Rafe was hooked. After the presentation he hung around and got to talk to Hugh. Hugh offered to take him up on a flight and that was the beginning of his lifelong love of flying. Hugh was that male figure that he needed, a strong, determined, forthright man who believed in him. Who told him that his dreams, no matter what they were, were worthwhile. Whenever he doubted his dogged pursuit of music, he thought back to the last conversation he'd had with Hugh. Hugh said, "I came up in a time, son, where the world boldly told black men and women that they were less than human, that we should be relegated to servitude, to the back of the bus. But we fought against all the hate, the push-back and the stereotypes to make history. You come from strong stock, son, from a people who lived and died for you to be here. So never let anyone tell you that you can't. 'Cause you can. You looking at the proof."

Rafe never forgot those words. He lived by them— maybe, at times, to the extreme.

Chapter 15

Avery still glowed inside from her time with Rafe, replaying every moment as she tidied up around the house before heading out to meet Kerry for a girl's night out. Just as she was preparing to leave, her cell phone rang in her purse. She pulled it out while walking out the door.

"Hello, Dad. How are you?"

"I'm concerned, that's how I am."

Avery's belly tightened. She knew all too well the tone in her father's voice and steeled herself against whatever his tirade would be.

"Concerned?"

"I want you to stay away from Rafe Lawson."

She stopped in her tracks. "What?"

"I know you heard me. Rafe Lawson is not someone I want my daughter associated with."

Her thoughts spun. "How do you…" The car parked in front of her house popped into her head. "You're spying on me!"

"I'm looking out for you."

"Looking out for me by having someone watch me? Are you kidding me, Dad?" Her heart pounded with rising outrage.

"I'll do what I need to. And I mean that."

She was so stunned words escaped her.

"I hope I have made myself clear, Avery. Stay away from Rafe Lawson. There will be no discussion."

The call disconnected.

Avery's eyes burned. Her hand shook as she put her phone back in her purse. She opened her door and stepped out, expecting to see the car parked out front. It was gone. Her father's domination knew no bounds. She got into her vehicle and could hardly think straight. How dare he? For her entire life she'd done everything in her power to please him. He had engineered nearly every aspect of her life for as far back as she could remember, from the schools she attended, the friends she made, right up to the profession she found herself in. Nothing was ever enough and now he'd amped up his reach by trying to manipulate her personal life. Having her followed! Demanding that she stop seeing someone! Her father had reached a new level of dictatorial manipulation.

I'll do whatever I have to. The words replayed in a loop over and over. She knew her father and when he set his mind to something there was no changing it.

She slammed the heel of her palm on the steering wheel as she fought back hot tears of hurt and anger. Her father was a powerful man. He could make her life and possibly Rafe's life a living hell. Of that she was certain.

Kerry had already gotten them a table at The Hub and waved Avery over when she walked in.

"Hey, girl," she greeted with a big smile. "I ordered us drinks 'cause I know we have lots to talk about." She paused and actually looked at her friend's expression. "What's wrong?" she asked, mildly alarmed.

Avery slid into her seat and dropped her purse next to her on the banquette. "I don't even know where to begin. You want the good news or the bad news first."

"Oh, damn. Give it to me. What happened?"

Avery lifted her apple martini and took a deep swallow then poured out everything, the good, the bad, the ugly.

Kerry muttered an expletive and slowly shook her head. "Your father is a piece of work. We both know that. I've been telling you for years that you have got to find it within yourself to get out from under his hold. I get that after your mother passed he poured his life into you. But you're a grown-ass woman now. You are entitled to live your own life. You can't spend it trying to please and win the heart of a man that cannot be pleased. The more you give the more he demands. Having you followed! What next, A?"

Avery had heard it all before. She knew every bit of what Kerry said was true. She knew that she allowed her father to run her life. But what Kerry never seemed to understand is how desperately she'd always needed and wanted her father's love and approval. She'd been so conditioned over the years that it was part of her DNA. Breaking free would be like losing a part of who she was. She knew it was crazy, but it was all she'd ever known. She was like a Stockholm survivor who after years of captivity identifies with her captor and ultimately shares the captor's beliefs, doing whatever she can to gain favor.

The waiter came and took their dinner order.

"So, now that piece of news is out of the way, how was your time with Rafe?"

Avery almost smiled. She pushed out a breath. "Like a dream…" She told her about his arrival, the talk they had, the time they spent together. "He's amazing," she finished on a soft note.

"Sounds like it. And I can't remember the last time I saw that look on your face or heard that tone in your voice when you talked about some guy you dated."

Avery lowered her gaze. Her cheeks heated. She could still feel his touch on her body, the beat of his heart against her.

"You have a decision to make, Avery. You can either collapse under the weight of your father's irrational demands or you can finally do Avery for once and be happy with someone that makes you happy."

Their dinner arrived.

Avery cut into her salmon. It sounded so simple, but she knew her father's veiled threat was real. There was no telling what he might do if she defied him. Being followed was the least of it. But then she heard the words that Rafe had whispered to her that first time they made love; *surrender to me*. She knew she'd already done that and she wasn't ready to let go.

She looked across the table at Kerry. "You're right. It is time. I want to be with Rafe. I have no idea how it will work with him living across the country, but I want to at least say that I tried. Whatever my father tosses my way I'll deal with it."

Kerry's eyes widened with delight. "There is a god," she said with a grin. "Good. It's about damned time. Take happiness where and when you can get it, girl, 'cause tomorrow ain't promised."

Avery lifted her glass. "To taking happiness."

"To happiness."

Rafe pulled into his driveway. He'd told Quinten he'd be in New York the following morning and invited him to Melanie's soiree. Quinten wanted him to stay at his place, but Rafe liked his alone time and opted to stay at a nearby hotel in the West Village. He looked forward to the trip. It had been a while since he'd been to New York. Years actually. The city that never sleeps still evoked painful memories for him.

However, the time away would do him good. He would maybe get his muse back, and, most important, spend some time with his friend, who hopefully could help him sort out what to do about Avery Richards.

There was no denying that she'd entered a spot in his soul that had been empty for a very long time. The feelings were not new but different in a way that had thrown him off balance. He'd spent so much time avoiding real involvement, genuine feelings that he was for the first time in his adult life uncertain. Uncertainty was an emotion that was totally foreign to him.

He wished he could say that it was only the incredible sex, but it was more than that. When he was with Avery, when he talked with her he felt truly alive, the way he did when he played his music or flew his plane or tore down the highways on his Harley. No woman had done that to him since Janae.

He shook off the memory. He didn't allow himself to go down that road, that's the only way he could make it through.

Rafe strode into the den, fixed himself a bourbon on the rocks and downed it in one long swallow. The warm burn seared away the memories.

He took the first flight out the next morning, opting for commercial rather than taking his Cessna. The almost three-hour flight was uneventful and he slept most of the way and was refreshed when they landed. Although he'd insisted to Quinten that he would get to his hotel on his own, Q was more insistent and picked him up at Kennedy Airport anyway.

"My man," Quinten greeted, giving Rafe their traditional hug and simultaneous handshake.

"Good to see you, bruh. You know you didn't have to do this, but I appreciate it." He draped his carryall on one shoulder and held his sax case in his other hand.

"Nothing to it. Come on. I parked in the lot."

They wound their way around the travelers waiting for luggage and strode over to the parking lot.

"You know Rae is ticked that you aren't staying with us."

"I'll make it up to her," he said, laughing.

"You sure will, 'cause she fixed dinner and no is not an option."

Rafe chuckled. "Can I at least stop at the hotel, drop off my gear and take a shower?"

"Seven o'clock."

"Be there."

* * *

They pulled up in front of the hotel.

"Thanks for the lift." Rafe opened the door and got his bag from the backseat. "See you at seven."

Rafe checked in and got settled in his room then took a shower to wash off the day. With a towel wrapped around his waist, he sat on the edge of the bed and picked up his phone. He stared at Avery's number, wondered what she was doing. He'd been thinking of calling her from the moment he left, while trying not to think about it at the same time. Yeah, some time and space would do them good—do him good, give him a chance to get his head right. He'd call tomorrow or the next day. That was soon enough.

It had been three days, going on four since she'd heard from Rafe. The last time she'd spoken with him was the day he left announcing that he was returning to Louisiana. Between the misgivings that she was having once again about the two of them, compounded with the ultimatum by her father, she wasn't in a good place mentally. Kerry's pep talk certainly had her reexamining her relationship with her father, and she'd come to accept that she had to do things differently if she ever wanted to be happy, but maybe that contentment was not with Rafe. She already lived her life on the edge. It was part of her job. She didn't need it in a relationship and it appeared that's the way things would be between her and Rafe. She was all for excitement and spontaneity but to always be in limbo with where she stood on the list of priorities was a problem for her. She'd lived her life that way with her father, much to her own detriment. She couldn't, with her eyes wide open, go down that road with anyone else.

"Ready?"

She glanced up. Mike was standing in her doorway. They were scheduled for the vice president's detail. He was making several stops with the first one in Dallas, on to Florida then back to DC. He was the featured speaker for Women Against Domestic Violence in Dallas, and the keynote speaker for Save our Sons, an advocacy group of mothers that had come together to fight gun violence in their communities and police brutality.

"Yes. Give me one minute." She shut down her computer, took her secondary weapon from the bottom drawer, grabbed her jacket and go-bag and walked out with Mike.

"Just saw Collin and Steven. They're going straight to the car. We'll escort the VP from his office," Avery said, slipping into her jacket.

Mike stabbed the button for the elevator. "We really haven't had a chance to talk since the meeting with the boss a few weeks ago."

"Hmm." She stepped on the elevator. "What's to talk about?"

"Both of us being offered the same promotion, for one thing. I'd say that would give us something to talk about."

She gave him a quick glance. "Funny, I feel the total opposite. Talking about it won't change the outcome. You do your job and I do mine. When it's all said and done the person deserving the promotion will get it."

Mike snorted a laugh. "You don't really believe that bull you just spouted, do you? When has the deserving person ever gotten anything in Washington? It's all about who you know, what favors are owed and who your daddy is."

Her head snapped in his direction. "Really? You're gonna go there?" She rolled her eyes. "My daddy doesn't get on the firing range for me, he didn't take my tests, put his life on the line to protect someone else, serve on any of my details. It's me!" She stabbed her chest, poking the Kevlar vest beneath her starched white shirt. "I got to where I am because I worked my ass off to get here and not because of Daddy." She tugged in a shuddering breath. He really knew how to draw out her temper.

"Look, I'm sorry. That was totally out of line."

The elevator doors swished open. Avery adjusted her jacket and walked out. The last thing she needed was to let Mike twist her emotions when she was on duty protecting the vice president.

They exited the agency headquarters on H Street and got in one of the three militarized Suburbans that would take the vice president to Air Force Two.

They would only be gone for two days. Normally that was a walk in the park, especially a domestic detail. But the idea that the time would begin with tension between her and Mike had the potential to make the two days feel like forever. She couldn't let his rhetoric or his masculine insecurities throw her off her game. She had to be on point every moment. It was bad enough that he'd been assigned to this detail in the first place, which was a last-minute call. Martin Palmer was supposed to go, but had come down with the flu. Mike was his replacement. Just her luck. But at least the time away would keep her mind off Rafe Lawson.

Chapter 16

Rafe accompanied Quinten to his studio with the hope of working on some music.

The short drive from Q and Rae's town house took them through lower Manhattan. The World Trade Center once destroyed by terrorists had risen like the phoenix to its former towering majesty.

The last time he was here was more than a decade ago. He'd come for a visit with Janae. She'd never been to the "Big Apple" and the trip was his birthday gift to her.

He and Janae Harper were students at Tulane, then Howard. Janae was a social work major, determined to bring good into the world through advocating for children in foster care.

They'd first met at an off-campus party. Rafe was playing with a four-piece band and Janae found her way to him after his set.

"Hey," she said as Rafe was packing up.

He looked down from the stage and he would have sworn that a halo glowed over her. He stopped what he was doing. "Hey."

"Great set. I've seen you around campus. Rafe, right?"

"Right." He took the three steps down from the stage and came around to where she stood. "And you are?"

"Janae Harper."

"Janae." He nodded his head. "Nice."

Janae was what is designated as petite. She might have been five foot five and a hundred and ten pounds soaking wet. She had the most luminous brown eyes that Rafe had ever seen. Her mouth was a perfect bow and when she smiled deep dimples carved hollows in her cheeks.

"I would have remembered if we had classes together," he said, taking her in. He usually went for the tall model types, but there was something about Janae that awakened a protective instinct. "You here by yourself?"

"No. I came with some friends but…I wanted to meet you before we left."

He glanced over her shoulder to see three young women huddled together checking them out. "Those your friends over there?" he asked with a lift of his chin. He sat on one of the tables and folded his arms.

Janae looked behind her. "Yes." She slid her hands into the back pockets of her jeans. "I should be going or I'll miss my ride."

"You live on campus?"

"No. But I have a roommate."

"Hmm. Well, I guess you better get going." He stood. "See you on campus, maybe."

She looked up at him. "Yeah, I guess." She paused. "Nice to meet you, Rafe."

"You, too." He watched her walk away. She cast one backward glance before walking out the door.

"Who was that?" Barry, his bandmate, asked.

"Some girl from the school."

"Cute. You heading home?"

"Yeah."

"We're set for the gig here next Saturday. But we'll meet up say Thursday to rehearse."

"Yeah," he said absently as his thoughts drifted back to Janae. He should have gotten her number. Tulane's campus was extensive to say the least. The odds of running into her again were pretty slim. "Need me to drop you off?"

"Naw, I'm good."

They walked out together.

"Hey, heads up," Barry said under his breath.

Rafe looked two doors down and Janae was standing there, or rather pacing there, looking a bit lost.

"Maybe you won't be going home alone," Barry teased and clapped him on the back before heading off in the opposite direction.

Rafe took a slow stroll toward Janae. "What happened to your friends?"

She brushed her wind-blown hair away from her face. "They left."

He frowned. "Just like that? I thought you were leaving with them."

She ran her tongue across her bottom lip. "I told them to go without me."

He studied her for a moment. "So…how're you getting home?"

"I…was hoping that you would take me."

He stroked his chin. His mouth quirked into a half smile. "Suppose I had other plans?"

"Do you?" she boldly challenged.

He chuckled. "Now I do. Where do you live?"

From that first night Rafe and Janae were inseparable. They did everything together from early morning jogging to discovering new recipes. She came to all of his performances and she dragged him with her to each "save the everything" event in the state of Louisiana. She was a dreamer, with a heart too big to contain, and she saw the silver lining in everything. Her enthusiasm for life was contagious and she was his biggest champion and fan. When she decided that she wanted to pursue her master's degree at Howard, Rafe didn't think twice. He relocated, as well. They got a place together in downtown DC, began to plan their future together—where they would live, careers, a family.

They were young and in love. Rafe was happy, happier than he'd ever been. His music was beginning to take off, Janae had a solid internship with the Department of Children's Services and was guaranteed a job when she finished her degree. She'd passed approval with his brother and sisters, his aunt Jacqueline adored her and even his father begrudgingly accepted that Janae was going to be a Lawson.

He'd made reservations for them at the Hilton Millennium on Church Street with perfect views of the Twin Towers, the iconic landmark of the New York

City skyline, Chelsea Piers, Battery Park and plenty of shopping.

They arrived in New York late in the evening, so rather than head out on the first night, they opted to settle in, order room service and enjoy the view and each other. The plan was to get up early and hit the ground running. He knew Janae wanted to shop but for later in the day he'd gotten them tickets to a play and he had special reservations at Le Cirque. He wanted everything to be perfect, for the perfect moment.

When Rafe woke up later than he'd planned and didn't find Janae in the room he wasn't surprised. She was notorious for getting up at daybreak to get her day started. Knowing her, she probably went out for a jog and to scope out some of the stores. He pulled himself out of bed, put on the coffeemaker and took a quick shower.

With coffee cup in hand he strolled over to the window to take in the landscape. Frowning, he stepped closer. There was a plane flying so low that it looked like it was going to run right into the building. Then the unthinkable happened.

Black plumes of smoke and flames shot from the window from the impact of the plane.

"Holy shit!" He could see the people on the ground running as debris began to fall from the building. He grabbed the remote from the nightstand and turned on the television. It took him a minute to get beyond the hotel advertisements to find a local news channel.

The reporters seemed, initially, to be as confused as he was and then the reports began to come in about a plane in Ohio that detoured from its flight plan and then, on live television, the second plane struck the

South Tower. The hotel shook. He could hear glass breaking and screams in the hallways. If there was any thought that this was all a freak accident, that idea was smashed.

Rafe tore off the towel and grabbed his clothes. He got his phone and called Janae. He was sure she would have come tearing through the door by now. The call went straight to voice mail. He tried again and again.

The chilling voices of the newscasters played in the background. He went to the door and pulled it open. Several hotel guests hurried toward the elevator. The doors opened. He knew Janae would get off. She didn't.

He tried calling her again. *All circuits are busy.* He never saw Janae again.

"How's your head?" Quinten asked as they got set up for their session, stopping the dark thoughts from swimming in Rafe's head. "It's been a minute since you've been back here."

Rafe blinked back the images, adjusted one of the mics and blew out a breath. "I thought I was past it, ya know." He frowned. "But I don't think it's something you get over. You can't, not really. I still think that if I'd picked any other place in the world Janae would still be here."

"Hey, we been down this road. Don't even go there. No way anyone on the planet would have expected what happened that day. Nothing you could have done."

"Yeah, yeah, I know." He took his sax out of the case.

"Well, when you *really* know you'll be able to move on." He gave his friend a direct look. "All the women, the living on the edge, the booze…" Quinten let the obvious linger in what he didn't say.

"It's the realization that there was no closure. I'd

planned to ask her to marry me that night." He shook his head. "Haven't been that close to taking the leap since."

"Look, I know better than anyone what it feels like to lose the center of your life. Man, I been there. My twin sister, Lacy, randomly gunned down. For years I carried around that guilt. If only I could have gotten us out of that neighborhood. If only." He sat on the edge of the table and folded his arms. "But when I lost Nikita, I knew my world had come to an end."

Rafe nodded slowly, remembering all too well the devastation that consumed his friend and threatened to take him from everyone that cared about him.

"But then I met Rae."

Rafe smiled. "Yeah, bruh, then you met Rae."

Quinten's eyes sparkled. "Changed my life, or rather brought me back to life. Didn't think it was possible. I was dead inside and wanted to keep it that way. Never wanted to feel that kind of loss. The best way to make sure that didn't happen was to not give a damn about anyone or anything." He pointed a finger a Rafe. "That's the space you been in for years, brotha. Only thing I can say is that at some point you're gonna want to do more than simply survive, you're gonna want to live."

Rafe's thoughts shifted to Avery. "Maybe. We'll see."

Quinten clapped Rafe on the back. "Avery is the one. Mark my word. And I swear I won't say I told you so. Now let's get busy. I been working on this piece and wanna see what you can do with it."

The session went better than expected and twice as long, but it was worth it.

"That's what I'm talking about, man," Quinten said

when they finally stepped outside. "That was live." They slapped palms.

"You're right. We should have done this a long time ago." He glanced upward. The white arch of the new Towers cut through the night sky. For the first time in longer than he could remember that sick sensation didn't roll through his gut when he saw the images, recalled the memories.

Quinten dropped Rafe off at his hotel and confirmed their weekend plans to head out to Sag Harbor for Melanie's get-together.

Exhausted but in a good way, Rafe flopped back onto the bed, and grabbed the menu from the nightstand with the intention of ordering before the kitchen closed for the night. He placed his order then turned on the television. The news channel was coming back from commercial and there she was. Avery was standing to the right of the vice president, looking very serious and crazy sexy in her dark suit, earpiece and stoic expression. He didn't even hear what the vice president was saying or make much sense of where he was. The only thing that registered was seeing Avery and realizing how much he actually missed her, and that seesaw feeling in his belly wasn't hunger, it was longing.

He stared at his cell phone and before he could change his mind he dialed Avery's number.

It rang so long that he was sure the call would go to her voice mail. Avery picked up, sounding like she'd been asleep.

"Hey," he said. "Sounds like I woke you."

"You did."

"I can call you in the morning."

"I'm up now."

He tugged in a breath. "How are you?"

"Fine."

This was going to be a tough conversation but he knew he deserved the cold shoulder he was receiving. "Listen, I'm sorry I didn't call sooner."

"Hmm."

"I, uh, came to New York, met up with Quinten. We laid down some tracks today. They sound really good."

"I'm happy for you. Listen, I have an early day tomorrow to head back home. Is there something in particular that you want, Rafe?"

"I want to see you."

"I don't think that would be a good idea."

"Tell me why?"

"Because it always leads to conversations like this one."

"I deserve that. But it doesn't have to be like this."

"I know it doesn't but you make it this way. You come into my life, turn it upside down, then disappear, leaving me with your promises."

"It's a little more complicated than that."

"Really?"

He heard the note of sarcasm in her voice. "Yes. And I want to tell you about it, tell you about everything."

"Rafe—"

"A close friend of mine is hosting a party this weekend in Sag Harbor. I want you to come with me."

"I don't—"

"I'll arrange for everything. All you need to do is say yes and pack a bag."

"I'll think about it."

"That's all I ask."

"I'll call you when I get back," she said, still non-committal.

"Okay. Travel safe."

"Thanks. Good night, Rafe."

"Good night, darlin'."

He tossed the phone aside. Avery had every right in the world to be upset with him. She was right. The reason why they were in the space they were in was because of him. He needed to give himself a chance to get beyond the walls he'd erected. Avery offered it to him. This time he was ready to take it.

Chapter 17

"Are you going to go?" Kerry asked as she walked alongside Avery in the corridor of their offices.

"I don't know. I mean, I was actually ready to finally say the hell with my father's demands and then Rafe pulls the same stunt." She shook her head. "I deal with uncertainty every day with this job. I always have to be hypervigilant, on the lookout. I don't need it in my personal life, too."

"I hear you. He did say he needed to tell you some things. Maybe he'll finally explain what's going on with him. Worst-case scenario is that you get a mini-vacation out of the deal."

"Very funny. I told him I'd think about it and call him."

"Do whatever you think is best for you, girl. I have a meeting. Catch up with you later."

"See you." Avery turned down the hallway en route

to her office. She was officially off-duty until the middle of next week. Getting away wasn't the issue. The issue was the on-again off-again actions of Rafe. If she was going to finally take a firm stand against her father and for herself, she didn't want it to be because of a man that she doubted, no matter how attracted she was to him.

When she'd heard his voice the night before her heart literally stood still. He had that kind of power over her without even trying. She was crazy about him, but she wasn't ready to risk the uncertainty that came from being in a relationship with Rafe Lawson. From everything that she'd read about him, he was unable to commit to anyone. And if she had any doubts he'd proved them to her up close and personal. He lived for pleasure. How could she ever hope to compete with that? She didn't want to be another notch on his belt, another tabloid headline, no matter how great the sex was or how whole he made her feel—when they were together.

When she got home she did what she'd been debating doing all day. She called Rafe. She wasn't sure if she was relieved or disappointed when he didn't answer. She left a message telling him simply that she wouldn't be going with him to Sag Harbor.

With that out of the way she settled in for a long relaxing weekend, even as she wondered if she'd made the right decision.

Even though she was off, she awoke with the rise of the sun as she generally did. She straightened up her bedroom, put on a pot of coffee, then went for her morning jog. She loved running when the world was still asleep and the light was beginning to peek through the treetops.

She ran for her usual half hour and by the time she rounded the corner to her street she felt renewed. She slowed as she approached her home and her racing heart had nothing to do with her jog.

Rafe was seated on her front steps. He stood when he saw her approach.

"Hey," he said softly when she stood in front of him.

"What are you doing here?"

"I got your message."

"I'm not going to change my mind."

"Don't want you to."

"Okay. So then why are you here?"

He squared his shoulders. "I was hoping we could talk and the phone isn't going to work."

She pushed out a breath and stepped around him to the front door. She dug in her pocket and took out her key. "Fine," she conceded. "Come in."

"There's coffee if you want some," she said while she walked through her open-floor layout.

"Sounds good. Thanks." He followed her into the kitchen.

"When did you get here?" She poured a cup for him and one for herself.

"About an hour ago. I left New York right after I got your message. Caught the last flight out."

She threw him a look, but smiled inside. "Must be important." She sat down. "So…what is it? What do you want to talk with me about?"

Rafe wrapped his long fingers around his coffee mug. He lowered his head, searching for the right words to explain what he'd struggled with for more than a decade.

"There was this woman…Janae," he began.

Avery listened, envisioning the woman who'd captured Rafe's heart, and her own broke as he told her everything from how they'd met to when he lost her and the aftermath—the guilt, the reckless lifestyle, his reluctance to become attached again.

"Until you," he said quietly. He looked into her eyes as she wiped tears away. "I didn't expect to feel the way I do. It shook me, reminded me that underneath the façade was an empty space. When you started to fill it, all I could imagine was that I would lose you, too. I figured the best thing to do was not let it go too far between us. So, I disappeared." He snorted a laugh. "But I can't stay away. Don't want to."

Avery sniffed. "You could have told me," she said gently. She reached across the space and covered his hand with hers. "I don't want you to stay away either."

"You sure?"

"Very. But no more secrets."

He nodded in agreement. "It's not always going to be easy for me getting used to this relationship thing."

Avery grinned. "Relationship thing, huh?" She slid down from her stool and stood between his parted thighs. She took his face in her hands. "What we have is brand-new for me, too. But I'm in as long as you are."

Rafe slid his arms around her waist and pulled her close. "I'm in."

Avery took his hand. "Show me." She led him to her bedroom.

When they finally emerged from her bedroom nearly two hours later they were both starved. They worked in tandem in the kitchen whipping up just about everything Avery had in her fridge. The island counter had an omelet, grits with cheese, biscuits, grilled turkey sausages, fresh fruit and orange juice.

"Since you declined my invitation to go to Sag Harbor, I have a better idea."

Avery lathered her hot biscuit with butter. "What might that be?" She took a bite and chewed slowly.

"I thought we could get away for a couple of days. Just us."

Her brows rose. "Oh?"

"I'm thinking Antigua. Stay at a resort, order room service, troll the beaches, hang out…make up for lost time."

She tipped her head to the side. A smile played around her mouth. "I thought we just did make up for lost time," she teased.

He leaned in and nibbled away a crumb from the corner of her mouth. He stroked her bottom lip with the tip of his tongue. Avery moaned softly. He snaked his fingers through the tumble of her spiral curls and pulled her in. "Oh, no, darlin'. I still have a lot of making up to do and it's gonna take a while."

"I don't think I have a bathing suit."

He grinned. "Even better." He kissed her slow and deep to seal the deal.

Clearly any kind of life with Rafe Lawson was going to be filled with surprises and extravagances that would make her eyes pop. He didn't do anything halfway. She was accustomed to a relatively good life and never wanted for anything. She grew up in a good neighborhood, traveled and went to the best schools. Rafe was on another level. But even though he lived the kind of life many only imagined, nothing he did seemed artificial or driven by ego or the desire to impress. It simply was the way he lived, and he had no problem lavishing that lifestyle on her.

They flew by private jet to the Caribbean island of Antigua and checked into the Les Palmier on Jumpy Bay, which overlooked the white beach and incredibly blue water. The five-bedroom villa came with its own chef, housekeeper and butler, Olympic-sized pool and indoor spa.

Avery dropped her small carryall on the gleaming wood floor and turned in a slow circle to take in the expansive rooms that were decorated in shades of white and rich carved wood with splashes of bright island colors on the throw pillows, artwork that hung on the walls and the sculptures that dotted the glass and wood tables.

There was a separate sitting room with a mounted television that was bigger than any she'd ever seen, comfy overstuffed furniture and a state-of-the-art music system. The chef kitchen was to die for and she could easily spend hours in the spa bathroom. The four guest bedrooms were impressive, but the master bedroom took her breath away.

The king-sized four-poster bed, decked in a thick winter-white comforter, mounds of pillows and cocooned in sheer white drapery, was straight out of a fantasy. A full seating area with a bar, an en suite bathroom and built-in drawers finished off the room, which opened onto an intimate balcony that looked out onto the beach.

"You like?" Rafe asked, coming up behind her. He lifted her hair and kissed the back of her neck.

"I... I don't even know what to say. It's incredible."

She turned into his arms and bathed in the warmth of his smile that lit a fire in his dark eyes.

"Whatever you want is yours," he said, his voice dipping down into her center. "This weekend is all about you."

"Is it?" she said and leaned up to kiss his lips.

"Anything."

"What are we going to do with five bedrooms?" she murmured, and fiddled with the belt buckle on his jeans and unfastened it. Unzipped. She stroked her tongue across his bottom lip while lifting his swelling member from the folds of his clothing.

"Test them all out, darlin'." Rafe's jaw clenched when her fingers wrapped around him. His right hand clawed through the back of her wild curls and pulled her fully into the possession of his mouth. With his free hand he snaked beneath her flowing skirt and was thrilled to discover that nothing separated him from his desire but air. He hummed in delight while he teased and coaxed her clit from its protective covering until it rose firm and hard. Avery trembled and gasped out loud when Rafe slid a finger inside her slick walls, then two.

Their kiss intensified as their bodies heated and dipped and curved into each other. Rafe kicked out of his jeans and shorts, pulled Avery's sundress over her head and tossed it on the floor, then feasted on her exposed skin.

Avery felt the telltale flutter in the pit of her belly, the trembling of her inner thighs and the sensation that everything was spinning wildly around her.

Rafe suddenly turned her around and bent her over the back of the couch. He hooked an arm under her belly, forcing her pretty rear end up higher, and spread her thighs with a swipe of his knee.

Avery cried out and gripped the cushions of the couch when the force of Rafe's entry shot the air out of her lungs. He groaned from deep in his gut as Avery's hot, wet walls sucked him in.

Rafe held her firmly against him as he moved deeply in and out, showering her back with kisses while he caressed her breasts and taunted her nipples. Avery rose up on her toes and lifted her derriere even higher to eagerly meet the onslaught of his thrusts. The mixture of their escalating moans and sighs echoed along with the tide that rushed against the shore again and again until they were spent.

Rafe and Avery had dinner on the balcony then went for a long walk along the beach. The night was exquisite. The midnight-blue sky was sprinkled with stars and the warm air blew gently off the ocean.

"How many times have you been here?" Avery asked.

"Hmm, a few."

She wanted to ask him with how many other women, but decided not to. If you looked for trouble you would be sure to find it.

"I've always come alone," he said as if reading her mind. "Great place to just chill and unwind." He squeezed her hand. "You're the first woman that I've brought to my private getaway." He leaned down and kissed her forehead.

Avery could have floated the rest of the way. "Why me?"

He slowed but didn't stop walking. "Honestly?"

"Yes."

"I don't really know." He paused. "All I know for sure is that I wanted you to experience this with me."

She glanced up at him, studied his profile in the starlight. Complicated. A mixture of contradictions. Hard, soft, distant, passionate, selfish, thoughtful, generous, reckless, protective, independent and needy. That was Rafe. For now, she was along for the ride.

Between making love at every opportunity, they did find time to tour the island and go speed boating around the reefs, which scared Avery half to death. They visited restaurants, historic churches and local shops. Rafe rented a car and Avery held her breath and kept her foot on an imaginary brake as they drove on "the wrong side of the street." Whenever a car came in their direction or they rounded a blind turn, Avery screamed and Rafe laughed.

"I'm going to kill you!" Avery cried as they tumbled into the villa, exhilarated. "You drove like a crazy person on purpose." She flopped down on the couch and pulled off her wide straw hat.

Rafe chuckled. "I wouldn't let anything happen to you."

"I've driven on the right side of the car before, but not on such narrow roads. And *I've* always been in the driver seat."

He chuckled. "Not so easy riding shotgun."

"Especially with you at the wheel." She tossed a pillow at him which he caught in midair.

He went to the bar. "Want something?" He fixed a tumbler of bourbon.

"Glass of wine."

He brought her glass of wine and sat down beside her. "Last night."

"Yes," she said with a sigh. "Then back to the real world."

"Hmm." He sipped his drink. "I'll need to head back to N'awlins."

"Sure. Of course." Her heart thumped.

He draped his arm across her shoulder and pulled her close. "I'll be back as soon as I can."

Avery nodded, but his previous promises rushed to the forefront.

"We still have tonight," he whispered and kissed her behind her ear.

Avery's lashes fluttered. She would focus on the now and leave tomorrow in the future where it belonged.

Chapter 18

Avery still glowed from her weekend with Rafe. And she wasn't going to let Mike's overbearing presence dim her shine.

"Looks like you got yourself a little tan," Mike said.

She ignored him.

They were assigned to accompany the vice president to the Capitol for a House vote and then to a dinner. The whole idea of having to spend her day with Mike Stone totally rubbed her the wrong way. But she had a job to do. That's what was important.

"Got out of town for the weekend?"

"Why does it matter to you?"

They walked side by side down the corridor.

"Only making small talk."

"I'd rather not."

They stepped outside, got in the waiting car and

headed to the White House to accompany the vice president to the Capitol.

As usual the vice president was in a great mood and as usual told very bad jokes for the short ride.

Mike and Avery exited the car first, as protocol, then ushered the VP into the Capitol.

The vote took all of two hours. For the most part Avery tuned out. Her thoughts kept jumping back to her weekend with Rafe, and in particular his phone call early that morning. He told her how much he'd enjoyed their time together and was looking forward to seeing her again…soon. He told her to have a good day "Secret Servicing" and that he'd call her later.

Inwardly she beamed. He'd kept his promise. There had been a part of her that was prepared for him to do as he'd done in the past—disappear. This time he hadn't. Maybe, just maybe things could somehow work out.

She went through the motions of her day, went home to change and prepare for the formal dinner.

The dinner was held at the Kennedy Center. Managing the crowd and the entrances and exits were the priority. Everyone had to be cleared to get in, no matter who they were.

Avery covered the right perimeter of the vice president, maintaining a visual of him at all times, even as he moved around the room. She spotted her father when he came in and hoped that he would keep his distance. The last time they'd spoken he'd all but threatened her and what she didn't need was to be distracted by her father.

"Agent Richards."

She turned. "Senator Lawson. Good evening."

"On duty, I take it."

"Yes, sir." Without being rude she refocused her sights on the vice president.

"My son came to visit me a few weeks back."

"Sir?"

"He mentioned that he was seeing you. Seemed to want to make a point of it." He smiled benignly.

Her cheeks heated but her expression remained impassive.

"Let me give you some advice about my son. He's a charmer. But he doesn't stick with anything or anyone very long. Just the way he is."

Avery's temples pounded.

"Your daddy and I go way back. Did you know that?"

"No, sir, I didn't."

"Hmm, maybe you should ask him about it one day." He glanced around the room. "I should mingle. It's the whole point of these things," he said in that deceptively soothing drawl. "You take care of yourself, Agent Richards. Thank you for your service." He strolled away as if he hadn't left behind several hand grenades waiting to explode.

Avery blinked rapidly to clear her vision and her head. What the hell was that about? What was his point? She lifted her chin and drew in a breath of resolve. She had a job to do. That must be her focus.

Mike's voice came through her earbud. "Father checking up on his son's girlfriend? Cute."

Avery inwardly flinched. Her gaze darted over to where Mike was stationed. A shadow smile framed his lips. She wouldn't dignify his comments with a response. Not here. Not now. But she would deal with Mike Stone once and for all.

The party seemed to last an eternity. Finally the VP was escorted back to his residence and Avery and Mike's duties were taken over by the residential security.

The instant Avery was alone with Mike as they exited the Suburban at the agency headquarters, she lit into him.

"I'm going to explain something to you so that we're real clear," she said and took a step closer to him. "What I do or don't in my private life is none of your business. None. I don't want nor do I need your commentary. As a matter of fact don't address me at all unless it's directly work related. Stay away from me, Mike."

His lips slightly parted.

"Don't," she warned, then stormed toward her car, got in and pulled off before she said or did something that would take this to a whole other level.

By the time she arrived home, her temper had been turned down to simmer. The freaking nerve of Mike! And Rafe's father? She knew he had to go out of his way to seek her out.

She tugged out of her clothes and tossed them wherever. Senator Lawson's words stayed in her head like unwanted house guests. *He doesn't stick with anyone or anything very long.* Everything she'd ever read about Rafe confirmed his father's words, but now she understood why and she believed him when he said that he wanted to be with her.

Confessing to her his greatest fear and his deepest loss wasn't easy, not for a man like Rafe. He allowed himself to be vulnerable, to trust her. She didn't take that lightly and she wouldn't let his father's veiled warning derail them before they got started.

She got in bed, turned on her side and switched off the bedside lamp. *Why did he think it was important to let her know that he and her father had a history?* And what kind of history was it?

Chapter 19

Rafe kept his promise and called or texted Avery each day that he was in Louisiana. He was back in the studio and the music was finally coming together. Although he wouldn't admit it out loud, simply hearing her voice and knowing that she cared about him and what he was doing was the thing he looked forward to every day. Her laughter filled him, her insight inspired him and her anecdotes about her days on the job had him laughing like he hadn't done in ages. He was slowly beginning to believe that he could be happy again, that he deserved it, and he wanted to share that happiness with Avery. Reconciling all that was still difficult at times. There were moments when he thought to pick up the phone and get with one of the women that had been in and out of his life just to get Avery out of his head. But something always stopped him. When he was alone at night he'd often tossed back an extra bourbon to take the edge off. But lately he found that talking with Avery before he turned in for the night was all that he needed. When he took his bike out for a spin the overarching desire to race into oblivion, challenge the laws of physics, was tempered. He didn't want to risk hurting himself anymore.

Rafe thought about all of this as he walked up the three steps to Avery's front door. He should have called first. But he wanted to surprise her. She'd told him the evening before that she didn't have to go in until midday. He was banking on that.

He rang the bell and waited.

Moments later the door eased open then swung back. "Rafe!" Avery beamed. "What in the world?"

That slow easy grin.

"I was in the neighborhood and figured…"

She grabbed him by his shirt and tugged him inside, wrapping herself around him.

He covered her mouth with a kiss. "Hey, darlin'," he said against her mouth and shut the door with his foot. "Damn you feel good," he dragged out.

Avery giggled. "Do you just hop in a plane on a whim?"

"The perks of having your own."

She shook her head in amusement. "You didn't say a word when we spoke last night."

"That would ruin the surprise."

She took him by the hand and pulled him behind her straight to her bedroom.

"You should call out today," Rafe said groggily. He turned on his side and spooned against her.

"Unlike some folk I have a job to go to."

He squeezed her breasts. "They would understand." He kissed the back of her neck and pressed his rising erection against her.

"Rafe…"

"Hmm?" His hand slid down between her damp thighs.

Avery moaned. "I…can't. I'm going to be late."

He stroked the slick folds of her sex. "Probably."

Avery turned onto her back. She looped her arms around his neck.

Rafe positioned himself above her and braced his weight on his forearms. He looked down into her eyes. Avery lifted her hips and tightened her knees against his sides as he slid inside her.

Rafe hissed through his teeth. The heat of her insides threatened to consume him. He could make love to her every day, every night and all the times in between and still want more. Avery peeled away his defenses and all those empty spaces in his soul were being filled. The fear that had lingered in his heart for so long lessened when he was with her. That realization more than anything shook him. He wanted to totally let go and surrender to her the way she had with him. And at moments like this when he held her, moved inside her, became a part of her, he almost believed it was possible.

Rafe watched Avery while she rushed to get dressed. He put on his clothes, as well.

"Coming for you after work today," he said from his spot on the bed as he put on his shoes.

She turned from the mirror.

"We'll stay at my place in Arlington for a few days. I'll drive you in."

She propped her hand on her hip. "Do I get a say?"

"Naw, darlin'. I want you with me and I need to be in my place for a while and I want you there."

Her heart thumped. "It's like that, huh?"

He got up and strode toward her. "Yeah, it's like that. Problem?"

Avery swallowed. His father's warning—that she had yet to tell Rafe about—and her own father's meddling, played in her head. But like Kerry said, she could either let others dictate her life or she could live it on her own terms. Besides, she couldn't think of anything she wanted to do more than spend time with Rafe. Him asking her to come and stay with him was yet another hurdle surmounted. She couldn't say no.

"I'll have to come here first and at least pack a bag."

"As long as it doesn't take too long," he said and kissed her lightly.

"Fine." She pushed him away. "I've got to go."

"I'm driving." He put his arm around her waist and they went out.

Avery subtly scanned the street looking for a car that was out of place on the quiet street and she spotted it on the corner. Her pulse pounded.

"Something wrong?" He opened the passenger door.

"Let's go. We'll talk on the way."

On the drive over to her office, Avery told Rafe about her father's ultimatum, and the comments that Rafe's father made to her at the dinner. Rafe didn't say a word the entire time, but she could sense the fury building in him by the set of his jaw and the way he gripped the steering wheel.

He pulled to a stop in front of her office building. She placed her hand on his arm. It felt like granite.

"Rafe. We'll talk later."

He nodded. "Yeah. I'll be here when you get off." He turned to her, flashed a half smile. "Go. You'll be late for real."

She leaned forward to kiss him, stroked his cheek and got out. Even as she walked to her office the nagging feeling that she should have waited to tell him continued to gnaw at her.

Rafe debated about going over to his father's office to confront him. But the reality was, he'd set the scenario in motion. He'd deliberately told his father about Avery to get a rise out of him, to stick it to him by dating his rival's daughter. And his father had done what Branford Lawson always did.

But Rafe's motives had changed. Yes, in the beginning he'd wanted to throw all kinds of roadblocks in the way of him and Avery. Sabotage them. Now things were different. Her father, on the other hand, was another story. Having people watch her house was on a whole other level of control.

He headed for the highway and called Alice from the car to let her know he was in town but that he wouldn't need her to do anything at the house. She assured him that the fridge and cabinets were stocked.

Before he headed in he stopped to pick up a couple of bottles of that wine Avery liked. On his way back to his car he slowed in front of a woman's boutique and decided to stop in.

* * *

Avery settled in her office, and was checking her email when her phone rang.

"Agent Richards."

"Director Fischer would like you to come to his office."

"I'll be right there."

"Hi, Catherine," Avery greeted the director's assistant.

"You can go right in, Agent Richards."

"Thanks."

She walked to the office door and knocked.

"Come in."

"Good morning. You wanted to see me, sir."

"Yes, please have a seat."

Avery sat in the chair opposite Director Fischer's desk.

"I'll get right to the point." He linked his fingers together on top of the desk. "A few weeks ago I spoke with you regarding a possible promotion."

"Yes, sir."

"As you know you are in contention with several other candidates. We haven't come to a decision as of yet. However, we've had to make some adjustments to your detail schedule."

"Sir?"

"The Security Council Summit is being held in Paris, as you know."

"Yes…"

He flipped open a folder on his desk. "You're being taken off the vice president's detail and reassigned to the Paris contingent. The meeting with the security detail is set up for this afternoon at two. The summit is set for at least two weeks. You'll be briefed on all the details at the meeting."

"Yes, sir."

"That will be all."

Avery stood. "Thank you, sir."

She vacillated between elation at getting to visit Paris, even if it was work related, and angst. If it was any other time she wouldn't think twice about hopping on a plane and leaving DC. The better part of her career was hinged on a moment's notice. It was commonplace to grab her go-bag and jet off to anywhere in the world. But it had been months since she'd been out of the country. Well, there was that trip with Rafe to Antigua. She smiled. This time was different. This time she had a reason to stay put. She had Rafe. They were in a good place or at least a better place and she didn't want anything to upset the balance. Not now.

Clearly she couldn't say no. That wasn't an option. This was her job, her duty, her career.

"Damn it."

The security meeting took longer than usual. There were more than one hundred agents that would be traveling to Paris to coordinate with the French security teams and the Direction générale de la sécurité extérieure (DGSE), the General Directorate for External Security. All the members of the US Homeland Security Council would be in attendance, as well as members from England's Scotland Yard. The goal was to bring the major powers together to coordinate strategies to fight further terrorists attacks. The one upside was that Kerry would be going, as well.

They walked back together to their offices.

"Two weeks in Paris isn't bad," Kerry said.

"Job has to have some perks."

"You don't sound too happy. I thought you were itching to get away."

"I was. I mean I am. It's just that me and Rafe… were finally getting to a good space, figuring out this long-distance thing…"

"Hey, it's just two weeks. Like they say, distance makes the heart grow fonder."

Avery lifted her brow. "Sure."

"Any more news on the possible promotion?"

"No. I thought it was what the director called me to his office for this morning, but it turned out to be this assignment. All he did say was that I was still in the running."

"That's something."

"True. Anyway, I'll catch up with you later. I have a laundry list of office stuff to take care of before I sign out."

"No problem. Chat later."

As promised, Rafe was waiting to pick her up after work. She was half expecting to see the dark car, but she didn't.

"Hey, darlin'."

Avery leaned in for a kiss and realized how happy she was to see him. "Hey, yourself." She fastened her seat belt.

"Ready?"

"Yep."

Rafe pulled away and eased into traffic. "How'd things go today?"

She pushed out a breath, leaned back against the headrest and turned to him. "I told you about the promotion I'm up for."

"Yeah. Wait…you got it?" He turned and beamed a smile at her.

"Not exactly. I'm being sent to Paris for the security summit."

"Paris! That's great. But why do you sound like it isn't? I know it's work but it's still Paris."

She shook off a response.

"What is it?"

She turned to him. "We are finally making this relationship thing work and…"

"Hold it right there. Look, this relationship thing *is* working. There's no reason for it to stop working in two weeks." He pulled over to the curb and stopped, unfastened his seat belt and unclicked hers. He cupped her cheeks. "This is your job. Just like music is mine. I don't want you to ever stop doing what's in your blood for anyone. Me. Your father. No one. I'll be here when you get back. Promise."

A hint of a smile touched her mouth.

He leaned in and sealed his promise. "We good?"

"Good."

He winked at her, fastened his belt and pulled off.

Avery settled back in her seat, then realized they were going the wrong way to her house.

"Remember I need to stop home and pick up some things."

Rafe grinned. "Not anymore."

"What does that mean?"

"You'll see. Until you have to leave, you're mine."

Chapter 20

"Rafe! What is all this?" His bedroom was lined with shopping bags.

"Should be everything you'll need. Take a look."

Avery went from one bag to the next taking out jeans, blouses, skirts, T-shirts, dresses and lingerie to rival Victoria's Secret.

"Rafe... I... This is too much." She held up the dress in front of her. "How do you even know my sizes?"

He crossed the room and plucked the dress from her fingers. "There's nothing about your body that I don't know, darlin'." He leaned in for a kiss. "Hungry?"

"For food?"

"Whatever?"

"I think I need to work up an appetite."

"Your wish is my command."

* * *

Rafe gave Avery a tour of the house and after a meal of grilled shrimp and fresh salad, they settled in for the evening. Rafe played a piece on the piano that he'd been working on. Avery came and sat next to him on the piano bench.

She placed her fingers on the keys and began to play the in-between notes that Rafe put down. The combination was perfect.

"Baby, baby," Rafe crooned. "You said you were ordinary. You are magic just like I told you."

Avery smiled. "It's been a while. But…it all came back."

He stroked her jaw. "Never left. You only needed some inspiration."

She rested her head on his shoulder. "Play something else."

He ran his tongue across his lips, settled his fingers on the keys and launched into a smooth rendition of "'Round Midnight."

"Thelonious Monk."

Rafe nodded and continued to play while Avery rocked to the music until it came to an end.

"You could just as easily play the piano as the sax."

"Hmm. I prefer the sax. The notes, the range. The piano is good for getting my ideas down."

"There's something that I need to tell you."

His brows drew together. "Sure. What?"

"The night that… At the Kennedy Center when your father spoke to me…"

"Yeah?"

"He said that my father and him go way back. That

they have a history. He made a point to mention it. Do you know what he meant?"

Rafe lowered his head, bit down on his bottom lip. He angled his body and looked at her. "Our fathers knew each other from college…"

Avery listened and her heart broke for her mother. Did her father ever love her mother? And he still carried a grudge all these years later?

"This is just… I don't even know what to say. It's like the Montagues and the Capulets."

He snorted a laugh. "Yeah, but in this version Romeo and Juliet are gonna walk off into the sunset." He kissed her forehead. "That's their issue, cher. Can't get caught up in it."

Avery looked into his eyes. "I know, but it's still hard to swallow."

He thought about his own fractured relationship with his father and the reasons behind it. How long is too long to hold on to past hurts?

Leading up to her trip abroad, Rafe and Avery spent all of their free time together. As promised he took her to and picked her up from work and they returned to his home in Arlington. The time between them was beyond anything either of them expected. It was easy and fun, they were in tune with each other's moods and needs.

Avery knew that she was falling hard for Rafe. There was no way to deny it and there was no turning back. She was all in. Yet she couldn't shake the echoes of doubt that sometimes crept into her subconscious and whispered in her ear that Rafe Lawson was still untamable. She noticed the sparks of restlessness in him, the faraway look in his eyes that he got at times when he thought she wasn't watching. When she would ask him what was on his mind, he would blow it off and say that he was thinking about a piece of music. Then there were times when he would go out on his bike for hours at night, only saying that he wanted to keep his bike in shape, and he would return quiet and subdued and his lovemaking was fierce as if he only wanted to block out whatever it was that haunted him. Those were the times that the whispers grew louder. Perhaps this time away from each other was what they both needed.

"I'll call you when I get settled," she said when they pulled up in front of her office building.

"Make sure that you do."

That smile.

"Are you going back tonight or in the morning? You didn't say."

"Tonight."

She nodded.

"Well, you better get going." He leaned over and cupped the back of her head. "You be safe."

"I will."

He kissed her long and slow and it shook away the misgivings that fluttered in her belly.

"I'll call you tonight." She opened the door and got out.

He popped the trunk, got out and came around to take her bag out. He stood in front of her and gently brushed his thumb along her bottom lip, leaned down and kissed the spot he'd touched. "Go," he said, his voice suddenly thick.

She grabbed the handle of her suitcase, turned and walked away. When she got to the door she stopped and looked behind her but he was already pulling off.

Chapter 21

It had been over a year since she'd been to Paris and the city of lights was as spectacular as she remembered. She only wished that she would have the time to explore, but their schedule was tight. They had to accompany the dignitaries from the US to all the meetings and stand at post during the hours-long meetings and escort them back to the hotel. She had to remain on call in the event that any of them decided they wanted to venture out of the hotel.

She'd called Rafe when she arrived and only got his voice mail. Her apprehension grew but then he called right back saying that he missed her already and wanted to know how the flight was, how her room was and what her schedule was. They talked and laughed as if he was only down the street and not a half a world away. She told him she'd run into his father on several occasions, but he was nothing but cordial.

They talked every night. It was the highlight of her day, but halfway through her assignment, she was called in by the Paris bureau chief.

"You wanted to see me, sir?"

"Yes, Agent Richards. Please have a seat. I've received orders from the main office. After the Summit is completed next week you are to be reassigned to remain here at the Embassy for six months. You will be relieving Agent Morrison."

Avery blinked in disbelief. "Sir. I don't understand. I'm supposed to return home next week."

"Circumstances have apparently changed. If there is a problem you will have to take it up with Director Fischer. The orders came from him. I'm sure he will be more than happy to explain further. It's out of my hands. You will be provided with living accommodations, of course."

He continued to talk but Avery had tuned him out. This couldn't be happening. Not now.

"If I can be of any assistance to you during your transition, my door is always open."

Avery focused on the bureau chief. She swallowed. "Yes, sir. Thank you." She pushed up from her seat and walked out.

As soon as she returned to her hotel room she called her father's office. She knew deep in her gut that he was behind this "change in her assignment." His secretary said that he was in meetings all day but she would surely pass along the message that she'd called. Avery called her father's cell phone and only got voice mail.

Then she called Rafe.

Avery had barely been gone a week and Rafe did everything he could to keep himself from thinking about her all day long. He'd thought that the time apart would do them both good. It would give him a chance to clear his head and try to figure out exactly what he wanted to do. If anything it did the direct opposite. All he could think about was when he would speak to her again and how many more days it would be before she returned. He never expected to feel the punch in the gut when she told him it would be six months before she was back in the States.

"Can they do that?"

"Actually, yes," she said and sniffed. "It's part of the job, but I know my father had a hand in this. There is no other explanation. I'm up for a promotion, so why station me here?"

He tried to imagine not seeing her for six months and couldn't. But he, too, had strings that bound him. He needed to be in the studio for at least the next month to finish up the album and then there was the editing and mastering.

"Listen, we'll figure this out."

"How?"

He pushed out a breath. "We will. Look, I'll talk with you tomorrow. You try and get some rest. Stay focused."

"All right," she said, her throat tight.

Rafe tossed the phone aside, stood up from the bed and began to pace. He walked to the window and stared out at the bright afternoon sun. He slid his hands into his pants pockets. When he'd first spotted Avery at his grandfather's birthday party, he was totally attracted to the physical woman. Their brief conversation and her apparent dismissal of him sparked his interest and curiosity. So he did what he always did—he went on the hunt, determined to capture the game. When he found out that there was a feud between his father and hers it spurred him to toss a match and ignite a fire. He'd even gone so far as to try to see other women, cut Avery out of his life, but he couldn't. The harder he tried the more difficult it became and he realized that he was fighting against the inevitable. She had seeped her way into his soul, made him feel again, made him believe that he could be happy again. And for the first time since Janae he was, and he no longer felt guilty.

He picked up the phone. He'd told Avery that they would work it out, and they would.

Avery and the other team of agents were in the hotel lobby doing a sweep before bringing through the committee members for the next-to-last day of their meetings. Her heart nearly stopped when she spotted Rafe at the reception desk. It took all she had not to run to him. He flashed her a conspiratorial wink and a smile before he was escorted to his room by the bellhop.

Avery could barely stay focused on her duties when all she could think about was that Rafe was here. The meeting dragged on forever and a day before her shift finally ended. Once the committee members were secured and their evening schedules verified, Avery, as casually as she could manage, went to reception and asked for his room number using her agent status to bypass the protocol of not giving out information on guests at the hotel.

She held her breath, knocked on his room door and waited.

Rafe pulled the door open and she would swear on a stack of bibles that all the lights in Paris had truly come on.

"Hey, darlin'," he said in that easy drawl.

She ran into his open arms and he lifted her off the ground and kissed her the way he'd been dreaming about since she'd left.

Finally he set her on her feet. She looked up at him and stroked his face. "What are you doing here?"

"Thought that was obvious," he teased. "I was in the neighborhood, figured I'd come see my lady."

Her heart raced so hard and fast that she felt giddy and light-headed.

Rafe pushed the door closed. "You done for the day?"

"Yes."

"So the evening is ours?"

"Definitely. At least it should be. I'm always on call."

"We'll go with the flow." He stepped back. "Let me look at you."

She laughed and did a slow pirouette.

"Hmmm. Definitely better in person."

Avery planted her hands on her hips. "Seriously, what are you doing here? You said you had to work on the album, you had deadlines…"

"Pays to have friends. I worked it out with the producers. They hooked me up with a studio here so that I can work on the tracks and not fall too far behind schedule. I do need to meet up with them in the morning and set up some time frames."

"I'm impressed." She sat down on the couch. "How long can you stay?"

"As long as I need to."

She crossed her legs and linked her fingers on her knee. "I need to ask you something."

"Uh-oh." He plopped down next to her and draped his arm along the back of the couch. "Ask."

"How can I put this? Um, I know that your family is…well off. I know that you have your own plane, you travel on a whim…your music is successful…but where does your money come from? I mean, you don't have a 'traditional' job, for lack of a better word. I mean other than your club."

Rafe fought to contain his laughter. "You starting to think I'm just a layabout?"

"No," she squeaked. "I'm just trying to understand."

He rested his head back and looked toward the ceiling. "My great-grandfather was a sharecropper for a wealthy white family in New Orleans. He was a hard and faithful worker. So much so, that when the owner died he gave my great-grandfather a parcel of land. He and my great-grandmother worked that land and bought some more. They were the first real black landowners in the parish. Between the land and the businesses he built a small fortune that he passed down. With each generation the family wealth grew. My father gave each of us—me and my siblings—our inheritance when we turned twenty-five. I guess I got some of my nose for the land from my great-grandfather. I invested in land development. It's not something that I announce to anyone for a variety of reasons, but I run two major development corporations. We specialize in affordable housing and rebuilding. Then there are the production companies that produce local musical artists as well as concert development and promotion. The businesses," he turned to her and grinned, "are doing very well. Then there are the investments…"

Avery stared at him in astonishment. "Why wouldn't you tell me all this?"

He gave a slight shrug. "No need. But now you know. Does it change anything?"

"No, but it explains a lot. So the studios, those are yours?"

He nodded with a sheepish grin.

Avery shook her head in amusement. "And the housing—how many developments have you worked on?"

"Several in the Lower Ninth Ward in N'awlins. One in Calcasieu Parish in Lake Charles, two in Baton Rouge."

"Does your father know any of this?"

"Probably. Not much gets past him."

"So if you're so successful on your own, why the animosity between you and your father? You not going into politics is that important to him?"

Rafe blew out a breath. "There's that," he said quietly.

"And...?"

He looked away. Slowly he told her about losing his mother, how deeply he was affected by it. He told her that he was the one that was at his mother's bedside when she died. And when he needed his father he turned all his attention to his career, all but abandoning his family. "It was the only thing that mattered to him for *his* sons," he said, his voice taking on an edge. "He wanted to carve a new family legacy in politics and anyone that wasn't on board got left behind." His jaw tightened.

Avery reached out and took his hand in hers. "Everyone grieves in their own way, Rafe. You...of all people should understand that. Your father turned to his career to hide his hurt and pain and loss. You turn to women, and drown your hurt in bourbon, and risk your life on highways and in the sky. It's how you deal with your own hurt and loss." She turned fully toward him and took his face in her hands. "You don't have to hide behind anything anymore." Her eyes stroked his face. "Not anymore," she whispered.

His nostrils flared and he rocked his jaw. The pounding in his chest intensified. He knew she was right. It was a truth that he'd struggled with accepting and still had not reconciled with it. He pushed up from the couch. With his head lowered he walked partway across the room. He kept his back to her.

"Why?" he asked quietly.

Avery came up behind him and slid her arms around his waist. She rested her head on his back. "Because I won't let you."

Rafe slowly swung around. The right corner of his mouth curved upward ever so slightly. "You're gonna have your hands full saving me from myself."

She ran the tip of her finger across his chin. "I work for one of the biggest, baddest gangs in the world, the US government. I protect people that sometimes I don't even like *and* I'm damn good with a gun. I think I can handle one…complex…stubborn…dangerously handsome…crazy talented…sexy man."

He bathed her in his smile. "So you think I'm sexy?" he teased.

She playfully slapped his arm. "I think I may need to check your sexy status."

"I aim to please," he said and pulled her in for a kiss.

Chapter 22

While Avery worked during the day, Rafe spent his time in the Paris studio location and even worked out a deal to play at one of the exclusive nightclubs while he was in the city to test out some of his new music on a live audience.

For months he'd struggled with getting his muse back. Now the music flowed from him like the air he breathed and he knew it was because of Avery. When he composed he thought of her and when he played she was in every note.

Unfortunately, they had to be very discreet with the time they spent together, so Avery generally waited until late in the evening to come to his room and left before sunrise to return to her own. They couldn't go out on the town together, but soon that would no longer be a factor.

It was the last day of the summit and she was officially off duty at the end of her shift. Before she started at the Embassy she had a week off and she and Rafe planned to explore the city together. He was scheduled to play a late set that evening and Avery looked forward to getting out and listening to him mesmerize the audience.

"I have to go," she whispered.

"What time is it?" he asked groggily and reached for her beneath the sheets.

"No. Stop," she giggled and swatted his hand away. "I have to get back to my room." She tossed the sheet aside and got out of bed, barely escaping his grasp.

"Are you going over to the studio today?" she asked while she got dressed.

He stretched and yawned. "Hmm, later this afternoon. But I should be back by seven."

She buttoned her blouse. "I'll be here when you get back." She leaned over and kissed him. "Stay out of trouble."

"Maybe tomorrow."

"Try harder." She hurried out, easing the door shut.

Rafe tucked his hands beneath his head and stared up at the ceiling. In case things didn't go well he hadn't told Avery that he'd contacted his father and planned to meet him later. When he'd called his father's room and told him that he was in Paris, Branford didn't seem the least bit surprised, almost as if he was expecting him. Rafe wouldn't put it past his father to know his whereabouts, and for whatever reason, for once, it didn't matter. In a strange way it made him feel kind of good to know that even though he and Branford had this fence between them, his father still kept an eye out.

Rafe slowly sat up. The past months had changed him, or rather the time with Avery changed him. He wasn't sure what the exact turning point was, the moment that he decided to give in. If he thought about it, there was no specific event. There were little things: getting to know her, seeing her willing to risk her relationship with her father for them to be together. She understood his past and it didn't matter. Instead of his past hurts and resentments pushing her away, it seemed to strengthen her and in turn it fortified him. He'd never dropped everything to jump on a plane and fly halfway across the world for a woman, or turn up on her doorstep to ask for forgiveness. Not even for Janae.

After losing Janae he didn't believe that he would ever love again. He didn't want to and fought it every step of the way, but he was in love with Avery. Of all the women he'd known she was the one that seeped into his soul and settled in for the ride. The realization shook him to the depths of his being and it felt as if a weight had been lifted from his soul.

But if he was ever going to be truly free he would to have to cut the tie that bound him to the hurt of the past. Avery was right. People grieved in their own way. His father chose to bury himself in work, built a wall around his emotions so that he would never feel the kind of loss he felt after losing his wife. He'd done the same thing as his father. As much as he'd tried to deny it, he was more like his father than he'd been willing to admit. It was probably why they always bumped heads.

He drew in a long deep breath. Making peace with his father. He shook his head in amazement. If they were as much alike as he was beginning to realize then his father would be ready to mend fences, as well.

He reached for the bedside phone, called room service and ordered breakfast to be delivered in an hour. In the meantime, he went to take a shower and get his day in gear.

Rafe sat in front of the television watching the news while he finished his breakfast. The reporter was outside of the Assemblée Nationale, where the French parliament was housed, which was now being used to host the security summit. She reported on the progress thus far, that this was the final day of meetings and the hope was that a full report would be forthcoming.

And then the world rocked right in front of his eyes. He felt the impact in his room. An explosion ripped through the building sending flames and debris into the air before the screen filled with static. He could still hear the screams behind the static-filled image.

What the hell had just happened? *Avery!* Frantic, he searched for the remote to change channels.

Cameras shook as frightened reporters spoke in rapid French.

Sirens wailed in the background.

Déjà vu. It was September 11 all over again. The fear, the panic, the sick sinking sensation that gripped his insides. *Not again.* Rafe grabbed his phone and dialed Avery's cell.

Rapid busy signal.

He ran to the door and tugged it open. Hotel guests poured out of their rooms, looks of terror etched on their faces.

He had to find Avery. He darted out into the hall to the elevator and started stabbing the button, willing the doors to open. Adrenaline raced through his body. He couldn't wait. He ran down the corridor past panicked guests and sprinted down the fourteen flights to the main lobby only to find it flooded with hotel guests and the Gendarmerie nationale, a branch of French police that was under the control of the Ministry of Defense. They were known to deal with serious crime on a national level and the fact that they had been deployed to the hotel told Rafe more than he wanted to know.

He pushed his way to the front, looked for a figure that exerted authority and spotted the captain who was dispatching orders to his officers to keep the guests contained in the hotel and to block off the exits.

Rafe spoke to him in hurried broken French. "I'm Rafe Lawson, Senator Lawson's son. He is the chair of the Security Summit Committee. I need to find him and Special Agent Richards."

"No one can leave the hotel, monsieur. The city is under lockdown until we can determine what took place."

"Were there any casualties? Did everyone get out? Can you at least tell me that?"

"I don't have that information, monsieur. Please. Step back."

"I have to find them!" he shouted above the din.

"Step back!" Two other officers came to his side.

Rafe held up his hand in submission, turned and headed back to the stairs. He ran back up the fourteen flights to his room. The television screen was filled with the destruction that had taken place. Smoke plumed from the building. Firefighters shot water onto the simmering debris. The entire scene looked like a war zone.

Emergency response vehicles dotted the street.

Medical personnel attended to people injured on the street. Sirens continued to scream while the reporters attempted to shed light on this latest tragedy.

Rafe's hand shook as he tried Avery's number again. *Rapid busy signal.* He turned in a circle, dug his fingertips into his head. Lee Ann!

He called his sister in DC.

"Lee Ann!"

"Rafe, where are you? Have you heard—"

"I'm here in Paris."

"What! Oh my God. Are you all right?"

"I'm fine."

"Have you seen Dad? I can't reach him."

"Signal issues here. At least, there is no way to get a call in to anyone that…" he sucked in a breath "…is inside that building. I need to get out of the hotel. But they have everyone on lockdown. Is there any way that maybe Sterling can make some calls, pull some strings?"

"Yes, yes," she said, panic rising in her voice. "I'll find out and get back to you as soon as I can."

"Thanks, sis."

"Are you sure you're okay?"

"I will be when I can get out of here and find…out what happened."

An eternity passed while Rafe paced the floors of his hotel room and tried to keep the ugly images out of his head. In between he continued to try to reach Avery and then his father, with the same results.

Finally, after more than two hours, Lee Ann called back to tell him that Sterling had been able to make contact with the American Embassy and the chief of police. As far as they knew there were no confirmed fatalities and all the injured had been taken to Val-de-Grace Hospital.

Sterling had arranged for an escort to take Rafe to the hospital, who should arrive within the hour to his hotel room.

"Please find Dad," Lee Ann said, her voice breaking. "And I hope whoever you're looking for is okay," she added, knowing her brother all too well.

"Thanks, sis, and thank Sterling for me. As soon as I know something I'll call you."

Rafe disconnected the call and continued to watch the horror unfold on the television screen. The knot in his belly tightened by the minute. Avery had to be all right and his father, too. He wouldn't survive it this time. He simply wouldn't.

There was a rapid knock on the door. Rafe nearly tore the door off the hinge.

"Monsieur Lawson?" asked the uniformed officer.

"Yes."

"Come with me. I am to escort you to Val-de-Grace."

"Merci." He grabbed his phone from the table, made sure he had his wallet and passport and followed the officer out and to a waiting police vehicle.

Armed police lined the streets, herding people back inside shops and homes. The cloying scent of smoke and burned metal tinged the air. All around him the sound of sirens continued to wail. His imagination went into overdrive as he envisioned bodies being taken away beneath white sheets.

Many of the streets were blocked off to traffic but the police car's swirling lights gave them quick access.

The car screeched to a halt in front of the hospital.

The officer who'd come to his hotel room escorted him inside, leaving his partner in the vehicle.

The officer spoke in rapid French to an officer who appeared to be in charge. He nodded.

"He will take you to someone who can assist you."

"Thank you for your help."

The officer nodded and hurried back out of the building.

"Come with me, Monsieur Lawson."

Rafe followed the burly officer who was further weighed down by his assault rifle, heavy vest and helmet.

They walked down the hospital corridor, darting around gurneys of the injured and the nurses and doctors that had to use the hallways for triage.

The officer stopped at the nurse's station and spoke to the nurse behind the computer screen. The officer gave Rafe a brief nod and walked away.

"How may I help?"

Rafe stepped up to the desk. "I'm looking for two people. They said everyone was brought here."

"The names?"

"Branford Lawson. Senator Lawson." He swallowed. "And Agent Avery Richards." His heart pounded while he waited for her to scan the information from the computer.

She glanced up. "Senator Lawson was brought in about an hour ago. He is being worked on in emergency."

His stomach roiled. "What about Avery Richards?"

"I'm sorry."

He gripped the edge of the desk.

"We have no information on an Agent Avery Richards."

"No information, what does that mean?" he shouted and tried to keep from leaping over the desk.

"All I can tell you, Monsieur Lawson, is that Avery Richards was brought here as a patient." Her eyes and voice softened, conveying the unspoken meaning.

His temples pounded. The air got sucked from his lungs. *No. No. Not again.*

"The emergency wing is down the hall to the right. Senator Lawson is in room 21," she said, breaking through the swirling fog that surrounded him. She handed him a visitor pass.

Rafe blinked rapidly. "Thank...you." He pushed away from the desk and managed to follow the signs to the emergency area. After several miscues in communication he was finally allowed to enter and was escorted by police to room 21.

He approached the partially curtained-off bed. At least three doctors and several nurses surrounded the body on the bed. Bloody clothes that had been cut from the patient were on the floor. A bag of blood and clear fluid hung from a hook above his father's head.

Branford wasn't moving and from his vantage point Rafe wasn't able to tell if his father was breathing. He couldn't recall his father ever being seriously ill or weakened in any way, not even after his mother died. This was surreal.

A nurse brushed by him on her way out.

"S'il vous plaît," he said, slowing her exit.

"Oui?"

"That's my father— *père.* How is he?"

"You must speak to *docteur.*"

She hurried away.

At the very least his father was here. He was alive and being treated. But the answer to the question that tormented him was where was Avery? He couldn't fathom the unthinkable.

There was a flurry of activity around his father's bed and two orderlies prepared to move the bed out of the room.

The doctor was first.

"I'm his son," Rafe said, grasping the doctor's arm.

The doctor looked at the visitor tag attached to his shirt. "He is going to need surgery to repair the leg. He has a concussion. Very lucky man."

The two orderlies pushed the bed out of the room and that was when he saw her seated in a corner in a wheelchair. She pushed up from the chair and their gazes connected.

The bed was pushed past him. He grabbed his father's hand. "I'm here, Dad, and I'm staying." Branford's eyes fluttered open.

"Son," was all he managed before he was wheeled away.

Rafe swung his focus back toward Avery and the relief that flowed through him was immeasurable. He strode toward her like a man in a dream and gathered her in his arms.

"Cher, cher," he whispered over and over. He couldn't find the words to express the emotions that swirled through him. *Sometimes we get lucky with a second chance.* Quinten's words came alive in his head.

Avery pressed her head into his chest and wept.

"It's gonna be all right, cher. You're here and I'm not going to let you go."

A nurse came back into the room. "We need to take her for scan for her head," the nurse said in broken English.

Rafe finally noticed the angry bruise. "Avery," he said, alarmed, gently pushing her hair away.

"I'm okay," Avery managed. "Something hit me in the head." She tried to laugh but winced instead.

Rafe wiped the tears from her cheeks.

"Please sit," the nurse instructed Avery.

Rafe helped her back into the wheelchair and walked with them to the scanning room. He held on tight to Avery's hand until he had to let her go.

Chapter 23

"Dad is in surgery. Compound fracture of his left leg. The doctor said he also has a concussion but he was conscious when they took him in," Rafe told his family on a conference call.

"Thank God," they echoed.

"And your friend?" Lee Ann cautiously asked.

"What friend?" Dominique wanted to know.

"Her name is Avery Richards," Rafe offered.

"She's there?" Justin asked.

"Yeah, she was assigned to the security committee detail."

"Wait, what? Who are we talking about?" Desiree chimed in. "Security detail?"

"She works for the Secret Service," Rafe said.

"So you went after her," his aunt Jackie chimed in.

For the first time in hours he smiled. "Yeah, Aunt J, I did."

"Good for you."

"Wait, I still want details," Dominique demanded. "Where did you meet her? And since when do you fraternize with Secret Service agents?" she asked with skeptical humor in her voice.

"Let's just get through all this and I'll tell you all about her. Promise."

"At least I can breathe now," Lee Ann said. "Dad is going to pull through and your 'friend' is going to be fine."

"Has there been any more news on what happened?" he asked of Lee Ann.

"From what Sterling has been able to find out, it is being deemed a terrorist attack. It was a bomb. President Montblac is scheduled to speak at a news conference relatively soon."

"Everything is still on lockdown," Rafe said. "So there's very little movement around the city. In any case I'm staying here at the hospital and I'll keep you all posted on Dad."

"Okay. Good," the family chorused.

"Stay safe, bro," Justin said.

"Plan to."

They said their goodbyes and Rafe returned to waiting.

Avery returned first. She wasn't going to be admitted as the CAT scan came back clear, but they did want to hold her for a few more hours just to be sure. She was placed in a room and Rafe was at her bedside.

"How are you feeling?" He held her hand.

"Achy but okay."

His eyes roamed over her face. "If anything had happened to you…"

She squeezed his hand. "But it didn't."

"It all came back, cher," he said softly. "That day. And all I could think about was getting to you."

She stroked his cheek.

"I couldn't imagine…that I didn't get to tell you… I love you, Avery, from the bottom of my soul, and I don't want to think about a day without you in my life ever again. Whatever I have to do to make that happen, I will. Whatever you want me to do, I'll do it. I've been running and running from this time in my life for too long, cher." His jaw tightened. "I surrender."

Tears filled her eyes. She blinked rapidly to keep them at bay but failed miserably. "I turned my trust and my heart over to you long ago, baby. I love you, Raford Beaumont Lawson. I love you. Always know that."

Rafe slowly stood and leaned over the rails of the hospital bed. His pulse raced. He could love again. Really love again. That acceptance was the freedom that he'd sought and finally found.

He lowered his head and confirmed it all against her lips.

"Monsieur Lawson."

Rafe tore his attention away from Avery. The doctor was at the door.

"Be right back." He gave her a quick kiss and stepped out of the room to speak with the doctor.

"I'm Doctor Pierre. Your father is out of surgery. The break was severe, but the surgery was a success," he said in halting English. "Of course because of the nature of the break we are concerned for infection. So we treat now to prevent."

"What about the concussion?"

"We will watch him closely. There does not appear to be any damage or bleeding."

"Can I see him?"

"He is in recovery. He will be taken to a room when he wakes up. Someone will let you know. I must go. Many patients today."

"Of course." Rafe squeezed the shoulder of the doctor. "Thank you."

The doctor offered a brief nod and hurried away. Rafe returned to Avery's room.

"What did the doctor say? Is your father all right?"

He pulled the chair closer to the bed and sat down. He brought her up to speed on what the doctor told him.

Avery let her head drop back against the pillow. "Thank goodness."

"Can you tell me what happened? How did you wind up with my father?"

Avery shut her eyes. "Everything was wrapping up," she slowly began. We were getting in place to begin the escorts." She paused, blinked rapidly as the terrifying images bloomed in front of her. "And then," she gripped the railing of the bed, "the first blast sent bodies and furniture flying. The sound alone was deafening and thick smoke filled the room. It was hard to see. People were yelling, screaming." The muscles in her face tightened. Her nostrils flared. "Training kicked in. We were there to protect our own." Her eyes squinted. "I crawled across the floor, checking the fallen."

Her lips pinched. "And…I found my colleague. Mike. He had a slab of wood…sticking out of his leg. I used his belt to tie it off and packed the wound with my blouse. He was in and out of consciousness, but stable, and I knew I had to keep moving. The smoke was beginning to clear and the enormity of the devastation…" She swallowed. "There were bodies everywhere. Blood."

Rafe squeezed her hand.

"We could hear the sirens. People started getting to their feet and helping those that were down. I kept moving and," she glanced at Rafe, "I found your father. A table had fallen on his leg. He couldn't move. I don't know if he was thrown and that's what caused the break or if it was the impact and weight of the table. I finally managed to get the table off him and I knew that break was bad." She took a deep breath. "He was barely alert but I couldn't risk anything falling on him before help arrived. The only shelter was that damned table. I don't even know how, but I pulled him under the table seconds before the second blast came. The wall behind us exploded and plaster and brick rained down. I guess that's when I got hit in the head."

Rafe gritted his teeth imagining the horror. "You're amazing," he said, his voice thick. "You probably saved my father's life."

Avery lowered her gaze. "It's what anyone would have done."

"I'm glad that anyone was you." He pushed out a breath and stood. "I need to find out if he's in a room yet, then call the family and let them know he's out of surgery. Hopefully I can see him. Then I'll be back." He lifted her hand and kissed her knuckle. "Try to get some rest, superwoman."

She gave a faint smile and nodded, even as her eyes fluttered close.

* * *

Rafe walked down the hospital corridor that had become even more crowded with the injured. He didn't see the doctor that he'd spoken with earlier so he found his way back to the nurse's station outside of the emergency area.

"Excusez-moi," Rafe said to the nurse.

"Oui?"

"I want to find out about my father. Branford Lawson. He had surgery." He spoke slowly, no longer trusting his limited command of the French language.

She held up a finger indicating that he should wait. She turned to her computer, typed in some information. "Your father has been moved to a room on the sixth floor." She peered at her screen. "Room 647."

"Merci." He headed for the elevators and checked his cell phone for any news on the attacks. So far no one had claimed responsibility according to the news reports. President Montblac vowed to bring the perpetrators to justice and return order to his city.

The elevator doors opened.

Rafe exited on the sixth floor and walked the corridor in search of his father's room. He stopped in front of the door. A nurse was by his father's bedside checking his pulse and pressure. Rafe stepped cautiously into the room.

"He's my father," Rafe said softly in response to the nurse's inquiry.

She smiled. "He is resting. Only a few minutes, please." She walked past Rafe and out of the door.

Rafe approached the bed and looked down at his father. His leg was in traction suspended by ties and metal. Rods and pins protruded from the white bandage that was wrapped around his leg.

He touched his father's hand. "I'm here, Dad. It's Rafe. You're going to be okay. You have to be 'cause you owe me a lunch." His throat tightened. "And I owe you a long overdue apology. You owe me one, too, but we'll work out the details when you get home."

"Monsieur Lawson."

Rafe turned. "Doctor Pierre."

The doctor approached the bed and checked the drip. "He will be asleep for a few more hours."

"How long will he have to be here? Will he be able to fly to the States?"

The doctor murmured deep in his throat. "We will have to see how the bone sets. Once he is fully stable, then—" he gave a slight shrug "—he can be transferred home. At least two weeks and that is because the trip is very long."

"I understand. Thank you."

Rafe returned to his father's bedside. "Looks like you might be here for a while. However long it takes I'll be here." He stroked his father's smooth forehead. "I'm going to call the family and bring them up to speed. But I'll be back." He took a parting look then walked out into the hallway.

It took several tries before he was able to get through to Lee Ann who connected the rest of the family that had all descended upon the family home. Rafe explained about the surgery and that it would probably be about two weeks before Branford could even be released to fly back home. But he assured them that he intended to stay and promised to call with any updates.

He returned to Avery's room. She was still asleep so

he went in search of some food and coffee. He found a seat in the cafeteria by the window. The swirling lights of the police vans and searchlights splashed across the night sky.

He sipped on his coffee as the events of the day played out in his head. How ironic that it was Avery who saved his father. Months ago he'd intentionally put Avery in his father's crosshairs with the belief that as par for the course his father would undermine the relationship, and Rafe could walk away guilt free. Yet it was Avery who'd saved them both.

Rafe went back to Avery's room. She was sitting up in bed.

"They said I can go," Avery said.

"Great."

"Did you see your father?"

"Yes. The doctor said he will be asleep for a few more hours. I'll take you back to the hotel."

"No. I'm staying here with you until your father wakes up."

"You don't have to do that."

"I want to." She looked into his eyes. "Don't you get that yet?"

His eyes sparkled. "Yeah, darlin', I get it." He leaned down and kissed her. "When we get out of here, I'm taking you home, with me."

"To Arlington?"

"No. Louisiana."

"What?"

That slow grin moved across his mouth. "There's some people I want you to meet."

Chapter 24

Avery was granted a short medical leave from the agency, and her reassignment to the American Embassy in Paris was postponed indefinitely; however, her promotion was almost certain. There were also rumors that she would receive a commendation. In the meantime, she remained in Paris with Rafe until his father was ready to be transferred back to the States.

As promised, Rafe was at his father's side every day and in the time they spent together, although under strained circumstances, Rafe and his father actually talked, shared meaningful conversation.

For the first time in their relationship, Rafe told his father about how he felt after his mother died and how his father might as well have been dead to him, as well.

"It's the only way I knew how to be, son," his father said from his hospital bed. "After I lost your mother it was like the light went out in my world. I was angry and lonely and I turned to my work."

"But what about us? We still needed you. I know I did."

Branford looked into the eyes of his son, eyes that were identical to Louisa's. "You kids were all reflections of your mother. Being with you all was a constant reminder that she was gone. It was selfish. I know that, but it was the only way I could wake up in the morning and put one foot in front of the other. I'm sorry, son."

"I get it, Dad," Rafe said quietly. "And I don't blame you."

Branford gripped his son's hand and for the first time in his life he saw his father weep.

Chapter 25

Branford sat up in bed, back at the Lawson mansion, surrounded by his sister, his children and his son-in-law, holding court like the king of the castle. It would be a while before he'd be able to get around but that didn't stop him from trying to run the committees he headed from his bed.

With grudging appreciation, Rafe watched his father in action, making calls, cajoling deals, moving pieces. Funny, his father was as much of a musician as he was. They simply used different instruments.

His sisters had pretty much kidnapped Avery since they'd gotten back, took her all over town and introduced her to the haunts of Louisiana. Rafe was sure his sisters took great pleasure in revealing whatever little childhood secrets that they could remember about their big brother. He figured as much because he'd hear them laughing and chatting until he stepped in the room and guilty grins were on everyone's face. He couldn't get much help from his brother, who only had eyes for his new lady, Bailey Sinclair, who seemed to fit right in with the Lawson mayhem. And Avery, who'd grown up as an only child, had found the sisters and family she'd always wanted.

In the interim she made peace with her father and got him to understand and accept that she was her own woman and he couldn't run her life any longer. She was in love with Rafe and if he couldn't accept that, then he couldn't accept her. She also told him that she knew it was him who'd set her up to be redeployed for the post at the Embassy.

"Even if it had worked out the way you planned, Dad," she said to him over the long painful phone call, "Rafe and I would still be together. We would have found a way to make it work. Because that's what people do for the people that they love. They make sacrifices. They don't try to keep the ones they claim to love from being happy."

"Sweetheart...when I thought I'd lost you..."

"But you didn't, Dad."

"Can you ever forgive me?"

"Did you ever love Mom?" she asked instead of answering.

"What?"

"Did you ever love Mom?" she demanded.

"Yes." His voice shook. "I did. Not in the beginning. But I grew to love her more than I'd thought that I could. And I held on to you so tight because I didn't want to lose you, too."

Avery wiped the tears from her eyes. "You couldn't lose me. Both of us are too stubborn to let go."

A beat of silence hung between them.

"When are you coming home, sweetheart?" Horace finally said.

"You promise not to have me followed or get me reassigned?"

"Promise."

"I'll call you in a few days and let you know."

"Good. And…bring Rafe with you. Looks like I'm going to have to get to know him."

Avery grinned. "I will."

"Um, how's Branford coming along?"

"Maybe you should call him, find out for yourself," she said softly.

"I might just do that."

"Talk to you soon, Dad."

"Soon."

Avery set down the phone on the nightstand. She turned and Rafe was leaning in the doorway, looking dangerously sexy.

"Folks are all downstairs," he drawled. His dark eyes sparkled in the light as he slowly strode toward her.

Her heart thumped.

"Heard some of what you said to your daddy." He set his drink down next to her phone.

She looked up at him, angled her head to the side. "What part?"

"All of it, mostly," he said with a smile. "But there was one part that hit me, right here." He poked his finger at his chest.

"What part was that?"

"That you loved me."

She teased her bottom lip with her teeth and slowly stood. She slipped her arms around his neck. "Really? Is that what you heard?" She brushed her lips against his.

"Hmm, sounded like it to me." He tugged her against him.

Avery gasped.

He threaded his fingers through her hair. "I hope that's what I heard." He slid the strap to her dress off her shoulder, and placed a kiss on her collarbone.

"It was," she said on a breath.

Rafe kissed her again. "Say it."

"I love you."

He lowered his head and captured her mouth and as always he was transported away from everything that held him to the ground. He had no idea how they were going to make this thing work—between her job and his career—but they would. He looked forward to it, the excitement and the challenge of it.

Rafe lifted Avery off her feet and plopped her on the bed. He pulled his shirt over his head and tossed it on the floor.

She slipped the other strap from her shoulder.

That slow smile eased across his mouth as he moved above her, bracing his weight on his arms.

She cupped his face in her hands. "Surrender to me," she whispered.

"I already have, darlin'. I already have."

* * * * *

Naomi shifted her gaze back to the stranger's, her palm
sliding against his as he shook her hand. The touch was
like silk gliding across her flesh, and she mused that he had
probably never done a day's worth of hard labor in his life.
"It's nice to meet you, Patrick," she answered. "How can
we help you?"

"I heard you mention the property next door. Do you
mind sharing what you know about it?"

She looked him up and down, her mind's eye assembling
a photographic journal for her to muse over later. His eyes
were hazel, the rich shade flecked with hints of gold and
green. He was tall and solid, his broad chest and thick arms
pulling the fabric of his shirt taut. His jeans fit comfortably

against a very high and round behind, and he had big feet. Very big feet in expensive, steel-toed work boots. He exuded sex appeal like a beacon. She hadn't missed the looks he was getting from the few women around them, one of whom was openly staring at him as they stood there chatting.

"What would you like to know about Norris Farms?" Naomi asked. She crossed her arms over her chest, the gesture drawing attention to the curve of her cleavage.

Patrick's smile widened. "Norris," he repeated. "That's an interesting name. Is it a fully functioning farm?"

"It is. They use ecologically based production systems to produce their foods and fibers. They are certified organic."

"Is there a homestead?"

"There is."

"Have the owners had it long? Is there any family history attached to it?"

Naomi hesitated for a brief second. "May I ask why you're so interested? Are you thinking about bidding on this property?"

Patrick clasped his hands behind his back and widened his stance a bit. "I'm actually an attorney. I represent the Perry Group and they're interested in acquiring this lot."

Both Naomi and Noah bristled slightly, exchanging a quick look.

Naomi scoffed, apparent attitude evident in her voice. "The Perry Group?"

Patrick nodded. "Yes. They're a locally owned investment company. Very well established, aren't they?"

Her eyes narrowed as she snapped, "We know who they are."

Don't miss SWEET STALLION
by Deborah Fletcher Mello, available September 2017
wherever Harlequin® Kimani Romance™
books and ebooks are sold!

Get 2 Free Books,
Plus 2 Free Gifts—
just for trying the Reader Service!

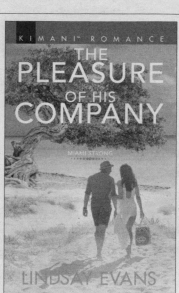

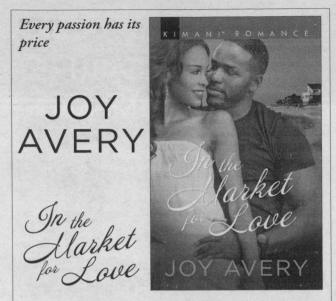

HARLEQUIN®

A *Romance* FOR EVERY MOOD™

JUST CAN'T GET ENOUGH?

Join our social communities
and talk to us online.

You will have access to the latest
news on upcoming titles and special
promotions, but most importantly,
you can talk to other fans about your
favorite Harlequin reads.

Harlequin.com/Community

f Facebook.com/HarlequinBooks

🐦 Twitter.com/HarlequinBooks

📌 Pinterest.com/HarlequinBooks

HSOCIAL